# Dangerous Accusation

"Flirting?" Robin's dark eyes flashed angrily. "Calvin Roth, I have not been flirting with Michael, and you know it!"

"Oh, yeah? So how come every time I see you together you're always laughing and joking and he's looking at you like he could die?"

"That's not my fault!" Robin almost shouted. "I can't help it if he likes me and follows me around and asks me out—"

"Asks you out?" Calvin stared at her. "He actually asked you out? So what did you say?"

Robin's anger flared. "For your information, I don't have any intention of going out with him. And I'm not sure about *you* anymore, either!"

**Books in the RIVER HEIGHTS ™ Series**

#1   Love Times Three
#2   Guilty Secrets
#3   Going Too Far
#4   Stolen Kisses
#5   Between the Lines
#6   Lessons in Love
#7   Cheating Hearts
#8   The Trouble with Love
#9   Lies and Whispers
#10   Mixed Emotions

Available from ARCHWAY Paperbacks

# River HEIGHTS™ #10

# MIXED EMOTIONS

## CAROLYN KEENE

**AN ARCHWAY PAPERBACK**
Published by POCKET BOOKS
New York   London   Toronto   Sydney   Tokyo   Singapore

AN ARCHWAY PAPERBACK *Original*

An Archway Paperback published by
POCKET BOOKS, a division of Simon & Schuster
1230 Avenue of the Americas, New York, NY 10020

Copyright © 1991 by Simon & Schuster
Produced by Mega-Books of New York, Inc.

ISBN: 0-671-73114-9

First Archway Paperback printing March 1991

10  9  8  7  6  5  4  3  2  1

Cover art by Carla Sormanti

Printed in the U.S.A.

IL 6 +

# MIXED EMOTIONS

# 1

"Robin!" Lenny Lukowski, owner of Platters Records, stuck his head around the stockroom door. "You still in there? You get those tapes yet? Let's move it!"

"Tapes?" Robin Fisher peered at him over the tall stack of CDs she was holding. "I thought you said CDs!"

"Nope." Lenny gave a huge sigh of exasperation. "Not everybody has a CD player, you know," he said, barely controlling his temper.

"I know. I just thought you said CDs, that's all." With the plastic-encased CDs balanced precariously in her arms, Robin looked around for a place to put them down.

The only good place was the floor, but she knew the minute she let go of them, they'd slip and slide into a messy pile. That would freak Lenny out. It took so little to get him going, and Robin wasn't in the mood to be yelled at.

"Here, Lenny." Robin carefully shuffled her way to the door and plopped the entire stack into his arms. "You take these and I'll get the tapes. You want the CDs out there anyway, right?"

"Right, but the customer's waiting," Lenny said, his chin resting on the top of the stack as he talked. "Don't take forever."

"Relax." Robin tucked her short dark hair behind her ears and grinned. "None of the other stores in town even have the new Bleak House album yet. If the customer wants it, the customer will wait five minutes."

Lenny rolled his eyes. "By the time we get our stock on the shelves, every record store will have them in and be sold out already." He started to go, then turned back. "You can find the tapes, right?"

"Don't worry, Lenny. I know exactly where they are," Robin assured him. "Go on, I'll be out in record time, ha-ha."

The buzzer over the outside door sounded, which meant another customer had come in.

Lenny raised his eyes to the ceiling and stepped back into the store.

For once, Robin did know exactly where the tapes were. When she'd first started working at Platters, the stockroom had seemed like a giant maze. She had almost caught on to Lenny's system, and now she rarely had to ask for help.

The longer she worked at Platters, the more Robin admired her friend Lacey Dupree. Robin was only filling in for her friend for a while so Lacey could have her afternoons free to visit her boyfriend, Rick Stratton. He was still recovering from a serious fall he had taken while rock climbing. Robin never realized how much Lacey did at work. She had to deal with customers and distributors, get ads into newspapers, make sure all the prices were marked right, and handle the stockroom, of course.

Two minutes had gone by, and Robin knew Lenny was tapping his foot already. Another minute and he'd be yelling for her. She grabbed the utility knife and carefully slit open the box of Bleak House tapes. Then she gathered up an armload of the cassettes and headed into the store.

"Here I am," she said, hurrying toward the counter. Lenny and the customer—a girl about twelve years old—were waiting. "Was that fast, or was that fast?"

Lenny didn't reply. He merely slipped the top tape off the stack. "I'll take care of this sale. You get the new display set up."

"Whatever you say, boss." Robin looked at the girl. "The man is a real slave driver," she said with a wink. "But his prices are the best in River Heights, and we're the only store with Bleak House's latest. Take my advice and tell your friends to hurry in before we run out."

"Oh, I will," the girl said. "Do you think you'll still have them tomorrow afternoon?"

"Tuesday?" Robin frowned a little. "Well, maybe, if your friends get here as soon as school's out. What do you think, Lenny?"

Lenny shook his head, amazed by Robin's sales technique. "Yeah, I think we'll still have some," he said.

"Better spread the word," Robin told the girl. She turned around and started toward the Bleak House display at the front of the store. Just as she reached the end of the aisle, she collided with another customer, a boy with reddish hair. The tapes, naturally, flew out of her hands and landed in a sloppy heap on the floor.

"Sorry," Robin said, kneeling down to pick them up.

"That's okay," the boy said. "It was my fault. Here, let me give you a hand."

"Let's work fast," Robin said, lowering her voice, "before my boss notices. He's got this idea that I'm clumsy."

The boy looked at her admiringly. "Maybe Mr. Lukowski needs glasses."

Robin glanced at him and saw that he was blushing.

"I mean, I'm sure you're not clumsy," he said quickly.

Robin grinned. "I am sometimes, but thanks anyway."

The boy's face burned redder, almost matching his hair.

"Haven't I seen you around?" Robin asked as they stood up and started putting the tapes on the display table. "You go to River Heights High, right?"

The boy nodded. "I'm Michael Quinn."

"Freshman?" Robin asked.

Michael stood a little straighter. "Sophomore."

"Oh." Robin hadn't meant to insult him. "Well, anyway, I'm—"

"I know who you are," Michael said quickly. "You're Robin Fisher. I've seen you in the halls a lot, and on the swim team, of course. You're really great."

"Thanks," Robin said, smiling. "And

thanks for helping me with the tapes. Anyway, what can I help *you* with?"

Just then, Lenny walked up. "Oh, good," he said to Michael. "You're right on time." Turning to Robin he said, "I decided to give you a little help."

"What do you mean?" Robin asked.

"Michael's going to work here. Not that you've been doing a lousy job or anything," Lenny said. "But with Lacey out, it gets a little crazy around here sometimes."

Robin laughed. "Don't worry, Lenny. I'm thrilled." She held out her hand to Michael. "Welcome to Lenny's sweatshop," she said.

"Don't listen to a word she says," Lenny warned Michael.

As Michael shook Robin's hand and smiled into her big dark eyes, his whole face seemed to glow. It was obvious that he hadn't heard a word Lenny said. All his attention was on Robin.

Ellen Ming was still at school, nervously pacing around the student council room. Lying open on a desk was the ledger she kept as treasurer of the junior class. Three times she'd reached for a pencil and started to fill in a number, and three times she'd stopped herself. Writing five hundred dollars in the plus column would be easy. But what would happen when they got the bank statement and it showed a combined deposit of only three hundred dollars? How was she going to explain the missing two hundred dollars?

Hearing footsteps in the hallway outside, Ellen quickly closed the ledger and shoved it in the desk drawer. The footsteps got closer, and a few seconds later Ellen's younger sister, Suzanne, burst in.

"Oh, good," Suzanne said. "I've been looking all over for you."

Ellen pushed back her shiny dark hair and tried to smile. "Well, you found me. What's up?"

Suzanne took a deep breath. "There's an opening on the student council for a freshman representative," she announced.

"Really?"

Suzanne nodded. "I've decided to run for it."

Ellen tried for an even bigger smile. "That's—really great, Suzanne."

"I'm so excited!" Suzanne said, spinning around and laughing. "Maybe I'm crazy. I mean, I know I'm hardly popular."

Ellen nodded. It wasn't that Suzanne was *un*popular. It was just that she was very shy, and had only a few friends.

"I think it's terrific," Ellen said. "I also think you've got a lot of guts."

"What do you mean? Because of Dad?" Suzanne asked. "But that's all over, Ellen. It was horrible when people actually believed Kim Bishop and thought he was a criminal. But now it's okay." Suzanne stopped speaking for a moment before asking, "How do you stand that girl?"

"I don't," Ellen said. "I just try not to have much of anything to do with her."

"Well, anyway, she was awful about that embezzling business," Suzanne went on. "She was so sure Dad was guilty."

Ellen sighed. It had been a terrible time. Their father, whose accounting firm worked for Mr. Bishop, had been accused of embezzling company funds. Of course, the entire Ming family knew he hadn't done it, and the culprit did turn out to be someone else. But Kim had spread her nasty gossip around the halls of River Heights High so fast that everyone, except a few good friends, decided Mr. Ming was an embezzler.

"But that's all over now," Suzanne said again. "Nobody's going to make any more snide remarks."

Not about Suzanne, maybe, Ellen thought. But what would people say if they knew two hundred dollars had disappeared from the proceeds of the tape and record sale? Two hundred dollars out of five hundred dollars that she, Ellen, was responsible for?

If only she hadn't locked the money in the student council room. But she'd locked money in the room before and nothing had happened. But something had definitely happened with this money.

Ellen would never forget how she'd felt— amazed, then confused, then panicky. She must have read the statement from the bank ten times, hoping her eyes were reading the bank's totals wrong. But there was no doubt about it—someone had stolen some of the junior class funds while the money was in the drawer. Ellen was terrified. If any kids found out, especially Kim Bishop, they'd automatically think she was guilty, just because of what had happened with her father.

Fortunately, the upcoming Hawaiian luau had been postponed. But pretty soon Ms. Rose, the student council advisor, was going to ask to see the books. The council was going to put on the luau and the junior class was donating the money. When either Ms. Rose or Mrs. Wolinsky, the junior class advisor, found out about the money, she'd accuse Ellen of being sloppy. Or worse, she might accuse her of actually taking the money. Ellen had no idea how, but she had to get that money back.

"Ellen?"

Ellen looked up to find her sister staring at her curiously.

"Are you okay?" Suzanne asked. "You seemed to be a million miles away."

"Sorry." Ellen shook her head. "Just daydreaming, I guess."

"Oh. Well, I guess you didn't hear me," Suzanne said. "I was asking if you'd maybe help me make some campaign posters."

Ellen frowned. Were those more footsteps she heard? Yes. Someone was definitely headed in her direction. Probably Ms. Rose.

"Ellen?" Suzanne said again, obviously concerned. "Are you sure you're okay?"

"I'm fine." Quickly, Ellen picked up her bag. "Come on, I'm ready to leave. What about you?" She had to get out before she met Ms. Rose. The woman might just ask to see the books to check on the money for the luau.

"Yes, I guess so." Suzanne followed Ellen to the door. "But what about the posters? Could you help me?"

"Sure. Let's hurry, though, okay?" Ellen said. "I've suddenly had enough of this place." Pulling open the door, she hung back a little to let Suzanne go out first. If Ms. Rose was there, Ellen could tell her she had to leave and that she'd show her the books the next day. By the next day, of course, she'd have to think up some other excuse.

It wasn't Ms. Rose, though. It was Kevin Hoffman, vice-president of the student council. During the trouble with her father, there'd been more than a few snide remarks that maybe Ellen couldn't be trusted as class treasurer. Kevin, who was something of a joker, had defended her, much to her surprise. If he found out about the missing funds, would he stand up for her a second time?

"Hey, you two," Kevin said.

Suzanne gave him a shy smile. "Hi, Kevin."

"Ellen," Kevin remarked, "you look totally beat."

"I am a little tired," Ellen admitted.

"I have a remedy for that," Kevin said, his eyes sparkling. "Pizza and a soda at Leon's. How about it?"

Ellen had just gone out with Kevin on Saturday night, and they'd both had a great time. But now she had had two more days to worry about the money and couldn't imagine enjoying a date now, at least not until she got this mess cleared up. Smiling, she shook her head. "Thanks, Kevin, but I can't. I'm just too busy—homework and everything."

"Sure, I understand," Kevin said, looking disappointed and very surprised. He obviously thought they'd be seeing a lot of each other. Ellen didn't want to hurt him, but under the circumstances she knew she wouldn't be good company.

"So, anyway, I was looking for Ben, but I guess he's not here, huh?" Kevin continued, recovering quickly.

"No." Ben Newhouse was president of the junior class and one of the nicest guys in school. Ellen knew he wouldn't suspect her of stealing the money, but she still hoped he'd never have to find out it was gone. "Why don't you try the *Record* office?" she suggested.

Kevin snapped his fingers. "Now, why didn't I think of that? Where else would he be but with Karen, the love of his life?"

Ellen smiled again. Her friend Karen Jacobs was crazy about Ben, and the two of them had finally gotten together. Karen would enjoy being called the love of Ben's life.

"Well," Kevin said, "if you'll excuse me, I'll be off."

Thank goodness, Ellen thought, as she watched him walk away. Now to get out of

there before Ms. Rose really did show up.
Biting her lip nervously, she pulled the door
shut and started down the hall.

"I think we should keep everything simple," Suzanne said, hurrying along beside
Ellen. "Simple but bold."

"What?" Ellen tried to shake her thoughts
away. "What should be simple?"

"My campaign posters. Ellen!" Suzanne
stopped in her tracks. "You really are out of
it. Don't you think I should run?"

"Sure I do," Ellen said. "Honestly. I'm
sorry, Suzanne. I've just got a thousand
things on my mind."

Suzanne nodded, but Ellen could tell she
was disappointed. Now she'd hurt her sister's feelings, Ellen thought regretfully, as
the two of them started walking again.

You have to talk to Nikki, Ellen told
herself. Nikki Masters was the only person
Ellen had confided in about the missing
money. Together, they'd gone to Nikki's
friend and neighbor, the detective Nancy
Drew. Nancy had been as helpful as she
could be, but she was too well known around
River Heights High to go undercover to in-
vestigate. If she started asking questions,
lots of people would probably find out about
the money.

Nikki had offered to help, and both she

and Ellen had been keeping their eyes and ears open. So far, though, neither of them had learned anything.

I'll call Nikki tonight, Ellen thought. Maybe she's found out something. And if she hasn't, at least I can talk to her about it. Missing the money was bad enough. Keeping it a secret was starting to drive her crazy.

 **2**

The phone started to ring just as Nikki Masters stepped out of the shower. She quickly belted her short blue terry-cloth robe, wrapped a fluffy towel around her head, and ran into her bedroom.

Grabbing the receiver, Nikki sank down on the colorful quilt on her bed. "Niles?"

"No, it's me, Ellen Ming," Ellen said. "Sorry."

"Don't apologize," Nikki said with a laugh. "It's just that Niles is coming over soon, and I thought he might be calling to say he'd be late."

"Do you have a few minutes?" Ellen asked hopefully.

"Sure I do." Nikki unwound her towel turban and shook out her wet blond hair. "What's up? Did you find out something about the money?"

"I wish." Ellen sighed. "Nikki, I'm going out of my mind. I know that money was stolen, and every time I look at somebody, I start getting suspicious. I hate this!"

"It's awful," Nikki agreed sympathetically. She knew Ellen hadn't confided in her parents. After what they'd been through recently, Ellen didn't want to upset them all over again. "I'm glad you told me about it, Ellen," she said. "I just wish I could be more help. But it's hard—you can't exactly go around asking people if they're suddenly two hundred dollars richer."

Ellen laughed a little. "It's not a great conversation-starter," she agreed. "But I know I locked that door, Nikki, and the only people who have keys are on the student council. I can't really believe that one of us did it."

"Listen, Ellen," Nikki said. "I know I promised not to breathe a word of this to anyone, and I haven't."

"But?" Ellen asked.

Nikki laughed. "Okay. But I really wish you'd let me tell Robin, at least. You can trust her, Ellen. She can keep a secret better than anybody I know. I think maybe we need some more help with this."

Ellen was quiet for a minute. Then she said, "I guess you're right, Nikki."

"Good. Listen, I've got to get ready for Niles, but let's eat lunch together tomorrow, okay?" Nikki said. "I'll make sure Robin sits with us, and we can tell her then. Don't worry, we'll put a barricade around our table if we have to, so nobody hears."

"Okay. Thanks, Nikki," Ellen said. "I feel better already."

"What are friends for?" Nikki said. "Hang in there, Ellen. We'll get to the bottom of all this."

After she and Ellen had said goodbye, Nikki plugged in her blow-dryer and dried her hair while she tried to decide what to wear. She and Niles were only going to the library—they both had research papers to work on—so she didn't need to dress up. She did want to look her best for him, though.

Not that she really needed to impress him, Nikki thought, shifting the dryer to her other hand. Niles liked her, she was sure of that. But was that all he felt? Did he possibly love her, the way she loved him?

Niles Butler was from England, and his father worked for Masters Electronics, Nikki's grandfather's company. Because Mr. Butler would be spending several months in River Heights, working on plans for expanding the company in England, he'd brought his family to live with him. Nikki had met Niles at a dinner party her grandfather had given to welcome the Butlers to town.

The first time she saw him, Nikki knew Niles was special. First there were his looks —thick chestnut hair and eyes to match. Then there was his accent, which all the girls in River Heights High thought was the sexiest thing they'd ever heard. Plus Niles was charming, and funny, and really into photography, just as Nikki was.

Nikki had recently broken up with Tim Cooper, and she hadn't expected to fall in love with anyone again for a long time. But she'd fallen in love with Niles in less than a week, which was probably a record—for her, anyway.

She still hadn't told him. For one thing, she'd had to be sure. For another, Niles had a girlfriend, Gillian, back in England. She was supposed to be coming for a visit sometime soon, but Niles hadn't mentioned her much lately, thank goodness. In fact, he'd never really spelled out exactly how he felt about Gillian.

Nikki was sure of how she felt about Niles.

Now all she had to do was get up the courage to tell him, and keep her fingers crossed that he felt the same way.

"I can't believe it!" Brittany Tate's younger sister, Tamara, was standing in the doorway of Brittany's room, gaping at the pile of shopping bags on the bed. "What did you do, rob a bank so you could buy all that stuff?"

Brittany tossed back her long, dark hair and frowned. "Don't be ridiculous," she said. "I do have a job, you know."

"Sure," Tamara agreed. "But since when does Mom pay you enough to buy three bags of clothes from Glad Rags?"

Brittany sighed. Of course she didn't make enough working at Blooms, their mother's flower store in the mall. Not that Mrs. Tate didn't pay her fairly, but it would take three times her wages to afford all the clothes she needed.

"Who are you trying to impress?" Tamara asked, twirling a strand of her own dark hair around her finger. "Chip, right? Chip the Snob Worthington."

Brittany sighed again. Tamara was only thirteen, but she was already good at sizing people up. "Look," Brittany said, "my feet are killing me. All I want to do is sit here for a while—in peace," she added pointedly.

"Okay, I can take a hint," Tamara said. She pushed her thick glasses up and grinned. "But you'd better be careful, Britty. One of these days you're going to wake up totally broke. Then the Snob won't have anything to do with you."

Brittany would have tossed a pillow at her sister, but she was too tired. Instead, she lay back on her bed and waited for Tamara to leave. When the doorway was finally empty, Brittany dragged herself up and shut the door. Then she collapsed on the bed again, using one of the shopping bags as a pillow.

Tamara was right, unfortunately. Brittany's money was running through her fingers like water. She'd borrowed her mother's credit card, with Mrs. Tate's permission this time, and charged the clothes she'd bought after school that day. That meant her next two weeks' wages were already spent. Her mother had been very firm on that point. The worst part was, she already had plenty of great outfits in her closet. She didn't need to keep buying more, and she wouldn't, if she were dating anyone but Chip Worthington.

The Snob, Tamara had called him. She was right about that, too. If there was a book about how to be a snob, Chip probably had it. In fact, he'd probably written it. A senior at the Talbot School, a stuffy prep school on the outskirts of River Heights, Chip Worthington thought he was every girl's dream come true.

Well, he's not mine, Brittany thought, kicking off her shoes and wiggling her toes. For Brittany, Chip Worthington was her ticket to the best social scene in River Heights. Her ticket to the most exclusive, expensive restaurants and all the best parties. Her ticket to keep up with her best friend, Kim Bishop.

If Brittany had to put up with Chip's ultrapreppiness and his superior attitude, then so what? It was what she wanted, wasn't it?

As her head sank deeper into her shopping-bag pillow, Brittany decided she'd better want it. Otherwise, she'd wind up broke for nothing.

Niles Butler, his dark eyes smiling, leaned across the library table toward Nikki. "What is it, Nikki? Do I look peculiar today?" he whispered. "You've been staring at me for ten minutes now. I'm beginning to feel extremely self-conscious."

Nikki blushed and shook her head. "You look fine," she murmured. Fine? He looked gorgeous, as usual, in a soft, teal blue sweater. "I was thinking about this paper. I guess my eyes just locked on you." That wasn't completely true. At first she'd been thinking, but the longer she stared at Niles, the more she thought about him, not her English paper.

"Well, I'm relieved that I haven't suddenly sprouted a huge crop of spots or something," Niles said with a chuckle. "How's the paper coming?"

"Slow," Nikki admitted. "Trying to find something original to say about *Romeo and Juliet* is tough. I think it's all been said a hundred times by a hundred different people." She shut her notebook and stretched. "But I'm almost finished, thank goodness."

Niles watched her. "I like that sweater," he said, still smiling. "You look great in yellow."

"Thanks," Nikki said, her heart thumping a little at his admiring tone. She wondered if she'd ever get tired of his compliments. Somehow, she doubted it. If they were seeing each other fifty years from now, her heart would probably still flip every time he looked at her.

"I could use some fresh air," Niles said. "What about you? Care for a stroll around the building?"

"Good idea," Nikki agreed, and grabbed her coat.

As the two of them headed for the door,

Niles reached out and took Nikki's hand. Her heart thumped in double time.

Outside, it was cool and windy, but the air felt refreshing. They walked quietly for a couple of minutes. Then Niles said, "Exactly when is this highly original paper of yours due?"

"Friday," Nikki said. "Why?"

"I was just thinking," he said. "My social studies paper is due then, too. Why don't we celebrate when it's all over?"

"Sure," Nikki agreed. "What do you want to do?"

"I was thinking about the country club," he said. "We haven't been to dinner there together—alone—since I first came to River Heights. Why don't we go Saturday night?"

"Sounds great. They don't serve pizza, though," Nikki teased. Niles loved pizza.

"True." Niles laughed. "But they do have candlelight." He stopped walking and put his hands on her shoulders. "I think I can give up pizza for the chance to see you in candlelight." Bending slightly, he brushed her lips with his.

Her heart was getting a real workout this evening, Nikki thought. Maybe a romantic, candlelight dinner at the club would be the perfect time to tell Niles that she loved him.

* * *

"Friday?" Brittany said into the phone. "It sounds perfect, Chip. We haven't eaten at the club in ages."

"Good," Chip Worthington said. "Actually, it might be Saturday. I'm still not sure."

"Either night's fine with me." Stretching the phone cord, Brittany walked to her closet and scanned the clothes she'd bought earlier that day. She'd have to choose between the blue minidress and the bright red velveteen pants.

"Good," Chip said again. "I'll let you know as soon as my parents have decided."

"Your parents?" Brittany asked, frowning. "You mean, they're coming, too?"

"It's about time they met you," Chip said.

He made it sound as if they'd be inspecting her, Brittany thought. And that's probably exactly what they would be doing. "Well," she said smoothly, "that'll be wonderful. I'm anxious to meet them, too."

"You might start thinking about what you're going to wear," Chip said.

No kidding, Brittany thought. "Of course," she said. "But this is only Monday."

"Right," Chip agreed crisply. "Just remember, these are my parents. And they're pretty traditional."

No mini, Brittany thought. No red velvet.

"Don't worry, Chip," she said sweetly. "I won't shock them or embarrass you."

"Right," he said again. "So. I'll let you know about which day."

"I can't wait, Chip. Goodbye."

Hanging up the phone, Brittany threw herself on her bed again. Just great, she thought. She'd spent a fortune on clothes that day, and not one of the things she'd bought was "traditional" enough to wear when she met Chip Worthington's parents! In fact, nothing she owned was right for the great occasion. She'd have to go shopping again. If she was lucky, she might find something that wouldn't put her over the charge limit her mother had allowed her. And that wasn't much.

If it were anyone but Chip, Brittany would have been insulted by the way he talked about her meeting his parents. As if they were royalty or something. Well, she *was* insulted, of course, and would have told anyone else to get lost.

Not Chip, though. Chip was too important, too rich, too right. Now all she had to do was get his parents' nod of approval, and then things would be perfect. Brittany would be exactly where she wanted to be—at the top.

**3**

"Are you ready for the test?" Calvin Roth, Robin's boyfriend, asked Tuesday morning as the two of them strolled down the hall.

Cal's green eyes were so serious, Robin couldn't help teasing him. "What test?" she asked, lowering her eyes a little to meet his. Robin was an inch taller than Calvin, but neither of them thought or cared about the difference.

Cal frowned. "Are you kidding? The chemistry test," he said. "You couldn't have forgotten. You *are* kidding, aren't you?"

"Of course I'm kidding," Robin said with a grin. "And of course I'm ready. When have I ever not been ready for a test?"

Calvin looked thoughtfully at the ceiling as

they walked. "Well, let's see. There was the humanities exam last month, that's one—"

"Okay, okay." Robin laughed. "Sometimes I'm not ready. But my grades are good—you have to admit that—and I am ready for the chemistry test." She didn't bother to ask Cal if he was ready. Chemistry was his best subject.

"How's Lenny?" Calvin asked as they reached Robin's locker.

Robin rolled her eyes. "The same. He thinks I'm scatterbrained and clumsy," she said, spinning the combination lock. "We're both counting the days until Lacey gets back."

As Robin pulled open her locker door, a carefully folded piece of white paper fluttered down, landing on her black- and white-checked high-top sneakers. Her name was printed neatly on it in blue Magic Marker.

"Secret admirer?" Calvin asked jokingly.

Not so secret, Robin thought, reading the note.

Dear Robin,

I had a brilliant idea last night. Since we're going to the same place at the same time today (Lenny Lukowski's sweatshop, otherwise known as Platters), how about if we go together? We could talk about how many CDs we'd have to sell to buy our freedom. Or we could talk about something else. Or nothing at all.

Michael Quinn, Esq.

Robin laughed and handed the note to Calvin. "Lenny hired somebody to help out at the store," she explained. "A sophomore. He's, oh——" She broke off. "There he is now."

Calvin glanced up as Michael Quinn hurried toward Robin's locker. His red hair was carefully brushed, his shirt was so white, it looked as if it had been whitewashed, and he was smiling eagerly.

"'Esquire'?" Robin said, when Michael reached them. "You didn't tell me you were an esquire."

"Okay, confession time," Michael said. "I just like the way *esquire* looks, so I thought I'd try it out." Turning to Calvin, he stuck out his hand. "Hi. I'm Michael Quinn. You must be——"

"Calvin Roth," Robin said as the two guys shook hands. Michael was really something, she thought, amused. It was obvious he had a little crush on her. She wasn't interested, of course, but it was kind of flattering.

"So," Michael said to Robin, "I see you got my note. How about it?"

Clearing his throat, Cal reached out and took Robin's hand. "The thing is, I usually drive Robin over to the mall," he said.

"Oh." Michael's face fell a little.

"Well, listen," Robin said, taking pity on him. "Why don't you ride with us?"

Michael's face brightened as if he'd stepped into a spotlight. "Hey, that'd be great!" he said happily, beginning to back down the hall. "Okay, then, I guess I'll meet you at the entrance to the parking lot after school. Good to meet you, Calvin," he added, still walking backward. "Thanks for the ride. Robin, I really like those earrings," he called. Then he turned the corner and was out of sight.

Robin laughed, shaking her head. Her earrings, abstract shapes in black and white, swung wildly like minimobiles. She glanced at Cal, expecting him to be laughing, too.

Not only was Cal not laughing, he wasn't even smiling. Squeezing his hand, Robin said, "Hey, what's wrong? You didn't mind that I offered him a ride, did you?"

"I guess not," Calvin said. "But I'm not exactly crazy about that guy. He's kind of weird."

"Weird?" Robin couldn't help laughing again. "Come on, he is not. He's just shy."

"Shy? He didn't shut up once," Cal remarked.

"That's his way of hiding it," Robin said. She squeezed Cal's hand again. "Michael's a sophomore, remember? He's not a supercool junior like we are."

"Right," Calvin agreed. "But I don't want to make a habit of giving him a ride every day, okay? He talks too much."

"Okay," Robin said. "I didn't know talking bothered you that much. You always call me a chatterbox."

"I know." Calvin finally smiled at her. "But you're not Michael Quinn, Esquire," he said. "You're my girlfriend. You could talk to me every second of the day and I'd never get tired of it."

"I'm going to remind you of that," Robin warned him, "the very next time you call me a chatterbox." Smiling, she leaned closer and planted a quick kiss on his cheek.

At lunchtime Ellen sat at an empty table in the farthest corner of the cafeteria, waiting for Nikki and Robin. She'd bought a salad, but she hadn't even bothered to take the plastic wrap off it. Her stomach was too full of knots to even think about eating.

"Hi, Ellen!" a voice called out. "Want to join us?"

Raising her head, Ellen saw Karen Jacobs and Ben Newhouse a few tables away. Ben, tall and good-looking, gestured for her to come over. "It's no fun eating by yourself," he called above the low roar of conversation.

Ellen shook her head. "I've got some cramming to do," she said, pointing to the book next to her tray.

"Chemistry, right?" Karen asked, making a sympathetic face.

Ellen nodded. Karen was her lab partner.

"Then we'll leave you alone," Karen said. "See you in class."

Ellen waved and stared down at the book. It was lucky she was good in chemistry, she thought. Her mind was so jumbled with concerns about the class money that the words on the page made no sense at all.

After a few seconds she glanced over at Karen and Ben. In spite of her problems, she found herself smiling. Karen was so happy with Ben Newhouse, she practically glowed. Especially in that beautiful jade green sweater that was fantastic with her hazel eyes, Ellen thought.

Ellen's smile slowly disappeared as she stared at the sweater. She'd seen it before, at an expensive store in the mall. It cost sixty dollars. And just the other day, Karen had worn a brand-new pair of butter-soft leather boots. The Jacobses weren't poor, but they weren't rich, either. Where was Karen getting the money for all these new clothes?

Suddenly ashamed at actually suspecting one of her best friends, Ellen's eyes filled with tears.

She wouldn't hate herself for suspecting someone like Brittany Tate, though, she decided, spotting Brittany. She was huddled with her two best friends, Kim Bishop and Samantha Daley. All three of them were dressed like models most of the time, but they'd always dressed that way.

A burst of laughter caught her attention, and Ellen dragged her eyes away from Brittany's group. Across the cafeteria she saw Sasha Lopez, dark-haired and popular, laughing with a bunch of guys. Serious about art, Sasha was always very dramatic looking. She usually dressed in black, with splashes of color—glittering red combs in her hair, or a fringed purple silk scarf tossed across one shoulder. Ellen had always admired Sasha's style. Now she found herself wondering how Sasha paid for all of her outfits.

Stop this! Ellen told herself. Who says the thief is buying clothes? And what makes you think it's a girl? It could just as well be a guy.

Just as Ellen began eyeing every group of

boys in the cafeteria with suspicion, Nikki and Robin arrived at her table.

"Sorry we're late," Nikki said. "I had to rescue Robin from the attentions of a lovesick sophomore."

Robin sat down and stuck a straw in her juice carton. "He's actually kind of cute," she said to Ellen. "If you know any sophomore girls who like red hair and gray eyes and a sense of humor, tell them about Michael Quinn."

"No chance," Nikki said, unwrapping a turkey sandwich. "He's not going to notice anybody as long as you're around. I saw the way he looked at you in the hall a few minutes ago."

Ellen tried to smile, but her mouth felt numb.

"Oh, Ellen, I'm sorry," Nikki said quickly. "I shouldn't be joking around."

"It's all right," Ellen assured her. "I keep telling myself that walking around as if I'm at a funeral isn't going to help anything. But I can't stop worrying."

"You do look miserable," Robin said bluntly. "Nikki told me something serious was up. What is it?"

"First you have to promise not to tell anyone," Nikki said. "Not even Cal. Not even Lacey. It's not that we don't trust them, of course, but the fewer people who know, the better."

"All right, I promise," Robin agreed. She leaned forward. "Why don't you tell me, Ellen? Maybe I can help."

Ellen took a deep breath and checked around her to make sure no one was close enough to hear. Then she quietly told Robin everything about the missing class money.

When Ellen had finished, Robin gave a low whistle. "Wow," she said softly. "Two hundred dollars."

"Not anymore," Ellen said. "Now it's one hundred and seventy-five that's missing."

Nikki frowned. "What do you mean?"

"I didn't see you this morning, Nikki, or I would have told you," Ellen explained. "But I went into the student council room earlier to get the ledger. I decided to take it home so no one would see it until this whole mess is cleared up. Anyway," she went on, "when I opened the desk drawer, I found twenty-five dollars in cash."

Still frowning, Nikki said, "Do you think the same person's starting to give the money back?"

"I don't know what else to think," Ellen said. "I was happy to see it, and I'm taking it to the bank right after lunch. No waiting till after school this time, not even for a minute."

Robin took a bite of her corn muffin and chewed thoughtfully. "I have an idea," she said after a minute. "If somebody's putting the money back, then maybe he or she'll keep doing it. We could stake out the student council room to see if we can catch the thief in the act," she said dramatically.

Ellen looked at her gratefully. "You mean you'll help?" she asked.

"Sure I will," Robin said. "Stealing's really low."

"And you won't tell anyone?" Ellen said. "You understand, don't you, why I'm so scared about people finding out?"

"Yeah, I understand," Robin said. "Kim Bishop gave you a pretty rotten time about your father. She'd have a ball if she ever found out about this, but she's not going to. Not from me, that's for sure," she went on. "Let's see, I'm still working at Platters, so I can't hang out after school. I swim laps early in the morning. Maybe you two can stake out the room before and after school, and I'll take a turn as often as I can during the day."

"Great," Nikki said.

"Thanks, Robin," Ellen said. "I feel better now that we have some kind of plan."

Nikki laughed. "Robin's good at coming up

with plans," she said. "I knew it was a good idea to tell her."

"It might take a while," Robin said to Ellen. "But try not to worry so much. One way or the other, we're going to catch us a thief."

 **4**

When the final bell rang on Tuesday, Ellen quickly left her class and hurried through the halls to Room 203, the student council room. It seemed impossible that the thief would pick this time to put more money back. There were too many people around. Ellen planned to stay for at least an hour. By that time, things would have quieted down and most of the students would be gone. Then maybe, if she was lucky, she'd see something.

The water fountain was a good spot, Ellen decided. It was about twenty feet from the door of the room. She could watch without being too obvious.

Pulling a book out of her bookbag, Ellen leaned against the wall near the fountain.

Lockers slammed around her and kids rushed by, shouting questions and tossing jokes at one another. Ellen barely heard them. As Robin had said, they were going to catch a thief, and that would take concentration. Nancy Drew would be proud of her, she decided. She was certainly keeping her eyes wide open.

Concentrating turned out to be harder than Ellen thought. She kept spotting people she knew, and most of them stopped to chat a minute. The first one was Lacey Dupree.

"Hi, Ellen," Lacey said, tucking a long strand of wavy reddish hair behind her ear. "I've been so out of it lately, I feel like I haven't seen you in years. How's everything going?"

"Fine," Ellen said, glancing over Lacey's shoulder at Room 203. The door was still closed. "How's Rick doing?"

"Great, really great," Lacey said. "I'm on my way to see him now. It won't be long before he comes home. I just hope he doesn't tear down the hospital walls first—he's getting really impatient."

"That's wonderful." Ellen tensed as Ben Newhouse stopped outside the student council room. Then she relaxed. Ben had just dropped a pencil. Ellen breathed a sigh of relief as he picked it up and walked away.

Ben wouldn't have taken the money, anyway; she knew that. She shouldn't waste her
energy worrying about him.

"Ellen?" Lacey's light blue eyes were curious. "Are you okay?"

"What?" Ellen blinked. "Sure. I'm fine,
Lacey. Sorry, I'm just not with it today."

"I know the feeling," Lacey said with a
laugh. "I've got to go. Catch you later,
Ellen."

The next person to stop was Karen Jacobs.
"Could you believe that chemistry test?" she
asked, running her fingers through her light
brown hair. "How do you think you did?"

"I'm not sure," Ellen murmured, her eyes
on Sasha Lopez. Sasha didn't stop at Room
203, either. Why should she? Ellen thought.
She's not even on student council. Then she
noticed Kevin Hoffman, but fortunately he
didn't see her. She wasn't in the mood to talk
to him because then she'd have to think
about their relationship. If they still had one.
Would they later? She forced herself to stop
thinking about him — at least until the money was found.

Ellen blinked a few times, and then noticed Karen still standing with her. She
smiled. "Are you looking for Ben? I saw him
just a couple of minutes ago."

Karen blushed. "For once, I'm not," she

said. She lowered her voice. "You know, I still can't believe he actually likes me. When Emily came back to visit for the dance, I thought that'd be the end, as far as Ben and me go."

Ellen nodded. For the longest time, Ben had been completely dazzled by beautiful, blond Emily Van Patten, who had moved to New York City with her mother. Emily's good looks had landed her a spot on a TV sitcom.

"Thank goodness Emily went home," Karen went on. "I know this must sound awful, but I hope she doesn't come to River Heights again for a long, long time."

Ellen started to reply, but she suddenly noticed Ms. Rose, the student council advisor, coming down the hall. "Karen," she said quickly, "don't think I'm crazy, but could you move a little closer and sort of block me?"

"Block you?" Karen laughed. "Sure, I guess so. Who are you hiding from?"

It was too late. Ms. Rose had already spotted Ellen. She was heading straight for them, a frown on her face.

"Oh, now I get it," Karen said, watching the tall, eagle-eyed teacher bear down on them. "What's she going to do, ask you to stay and work?"

"Probably," Ellen said, even though she thought she knew exactly what Ms. Rose was going to say.

"Well, I've got to get to the *Record* office," Karen said. She was the layout editor for the student newspaper. "Don't let Ms. Rose talk you into doing anything extra," she added as she moved away. "You work hard enough for two people."

Ellen smiled nervously and then braced herself. Sure enough, the minute Ms. Rose reached her, she said, "I've been looking for you all day, Ellen. I was in the student council room earlier, and I noticed that the junior class ledger book was gone."

"Oh, y-yes," Ellen stammered. "I thought I'd take it home today." Fortunately she'd already put the heavy book in her locker. "I just can't seem to find the time to work on it here."

Ms. Rose's frown deepened. "You mean it's not up to date yet?"

"Not quite," Ellen admitted. "But it won't take me long."

"Well, please see that it doesn't," Ms. Rose said crisply. "It's important to know exactly how much you have in that account so we can start planning the student council luau."

"Right," Ellen agreed, hoping she sounded as concerned and serious as Ms. Rose. "I'll get it done before the next meeting. You can count on it."

Now what am I going to do? Ellen thought frantically as the teacher marched off down the hall. The next meeting was only a week away. If she didn't find the missing money before then, she'd have to admit everything to the junior-class officers and the entire student council.

While Ellen was keeping watch on Room 203, Calvin Roth was trying to keep his eyes on the road. It wasn't easy—not with Michael Quinn bobbing forward from the back seat every few seconds to say something to Robin. Every time his head came between Cal and Robin, Cal felt like giving him a shot with his elbow.

"So tell me, Robin," Michael said, leaning forward for at least the tenth time, "what's it really like having Lenny Lukowski for a boss? I don't know what to expect."

"Lenny's okay," Robin said, turning sideways in the front seat. "He's cheap, so don't expect a raise for at least a decade or two."

Michael laughed loudly, right in Calvin's ear.

"He likes everything to run smoothly," Robin went on. "And he's kind of nervous, so the least little mistake freaks him out. He doesn't hold a grudge, though, thank heavens," she added. "If he did, I would have been fired my first day on the job."

"You mean you make mistakes?" Michael asked. "I don't believe it."

"Believe it," Robin said dryly. "You saw me drop those tapes yesterday. That's the kind of thing that drives Lenny up the wall. And I'm always doing stuff like that."

"Oh, I bet you're exaggerating."

The admiration in Michael's voice made Calvin feel like gagging. How could this guy—a sophomore, no less—actually sit in Calvin's car and try to hit on Calvin's girl?

Robin didn't seem to mind, Calvin noticed. In fact, she seemed to be enjoying it, which really bothered him. He knew she wasn't interested in this guy. So why didn't she just give him a not-so-subtle hint to back off?

"Well," Michael was saying, "if you *do* mess up again, don't panic. I'll distract Lenny while you clean up. I'm good at distracting people."

That's for sure, Calvin thought. Clearing his throat, he said, "Listen, Mike—"

"Michael," the boy said. "I've never been called Mike. Not that I really mind, but I'm just not used to it."

"Right," Calvin said. "Well, listen, you

want to sit back and put your seat belt on?
The traffic really gets thick around the mall."

"Oh, sure. No problem, Cal."

Michael finally settled himself in the back
seat, and Calvin glanced at him in the rearview mirror. "Thanks, Mike," he said.

By four o'clock the hall outside Room 203
was completely empty. It had been that way
for twenty minutes. Ellen decided to call it
quits for the day. Even if the thief came now,
he or she wouldn't dare do anything. Not
with Ellen standing guard next to the water
fountain.

Walking home slowly, Ellen hardly noticed the chilly wind blowing in her face and
whipping her chin-length dark hair into a
mass of tangles. She knew she shouldn't feel
so disappointed. After all, Nancy Drew had
told her and Nikki that she'd often spent
days watching for suspects without anything
happening. Ellen had only spent a couple of
hours watching the student council room so
far.

Still, she'd been wishing so hard for something to happen that she couldn't help feeling
let down.

"Hey, Ellen!" a voice called out, startling
her. "Want a ride?"

Ellen turned and saw Kevin Hoffman driving slowly beside her in an old subcompact. She wouldn't have minded a ride, but she still wasn't up to facing him.

"No thanks," she said with a smile. "I need to walk."

Kevin kept his car even with her. "You sure?" he asked. "I see you've got that ledger with you. It looks pretty heavy. Must be all that money we raked in from the record and tape sale, right?"

"That's right," Ellen said, forcing a smile.

"Well, come on, get in," Kevin said. "We can talk about what the class should do with all that money. What is it, anyway? About five hundred?"

"Listen, Kevin," Ellen said, "I appreciate the offer, but I'd really rather walk."

"Okay." Kevin seemed very disappointed, but he tried to recover and gave her a smile. "Catch you tomorrow, Ellen," he said softly.

Ellen watched Kevin's car disappear around a corner. Kevin had never seemed that interested in the class money before, she thought. And how did he know how much they'd taken in from the record and tape sale?

Of course, Ben Newhouse could have told him. Ben was the only other person who might know. Or maybe Kevin had just been guessing. He liked being the class clown and joker, but he was also a really nice guy. Ellen had had a crush on him for ages and really couldn't believe he was a thief. But then, Ellen couldn't believe that *anyone* she knew was a thief. Kevin was student council vice-president and he did have a key to Room 203. . . .

Ellen was surprised that she had made it to her house already and trudged up the sidewalk to the front door, still lost in thought.

"There you are," Mrs. Ming said when Ellen walked in. "I was beginning to get a little worried."

"I'm sorry, Mom," Ellen answered. "I would have called but didn't know you were going to be home early today."

"Hi, Ellen," Suzanne said, coming out of the kitchen with a can of soda in her hand. "I just told Mom that I'm running for freshman student council. She thinks it's great."

"I really do," Mrs. Ming agreed with a smile. "You two girls are certainly going to make your mark at River Heights High. Your father and I are very proud of you both."

"I have to win first, Mom," Suzanne said.

"But I think I have a good chance." She turned to Ellen. "Do you think we could talk about the posters now?"

The posters. Ellen had completely forgotten. "Oh, Suzanne, I'm sorry," she said, holding out the books she was carrying. "I've got a ton of work. I might be able to help you later tonight, but I'm not sure."

"Okay." Suzanne was obviously disappointed. "But I've got to get them done soon. I mean, Alice Watson's putting hers up tomorrow, and she's my biggest competition."

"I can't help it," Ellen almost snapped. "I have to do my homework first!"

"All right already," Suzanne murmured.

Ellen sighed, ashamed of herself. "I'm sorry," she said softly. "I'll help you if I can."

As she walked down the hall to her bedroom, Ellen could almost feel her mother and sister watching her. She knew they were surprised and hurt by her moodiness. And why shouldn't they be? They had no idea what was bothering her.

Ellen knew she should tell them, but she just couldn't bring herself to do it. She'd always been so responsible. She'd never even lost her lunch money—not once, not even in the first grade. How could she explain that she'd let two hundred dollars—one hundred seventy-five now—disappear?

Flinging herself down on her bed, Ellen closed her eyes and pushed the hurt look on Suzanne's face out of her mind. She couldn't think about that now. She had to concentrate on the missing money. Time was running out.

 **5**

On Wednesday morning Brittany slid proudly into the passenger seat of Chip Worthington's snappy British sports car. Riding in the green Jaguar always made her feel great. Jeremy Pratt, Kim's boyfriend, had a Porsche, but Chip said that Porsches were common. Brittany wasn't sure about that— she certainly wouldn't mind having one— but Chip's sleek sports car was perfectly all right, too.

"So," she said as they sped away from her house, "do you know whether we'll be going to the club on Friday or Saturday?"

"Saturday, for sure," Chip said, adjusting his striped school tie with one hand. "My father won't get back from his business trip till Friday night."

Good, Brittany thought. She'd have one more day to find an outfit.

Chip flashed her a smile, his perfectly even white teeth gleaming. "I mentioned that it was kind of formal, didn't I?"

"You didn't have to," Brittany said smoothly, wondering exactly what he meant by "formal." "I expected to dress up, naturally."

"Good." As he pulled to a stop at a light, Chip quickly checked his reflection in his visor mirror. Running a hand over his straight brown hair, he said, "My mother won't be wearing a long dress, or anything like that, of course."

"Of course." Brittany knew that much, for crying out loud. Nobody wore long dresses to the club, unless there was a dance. Chip had a habit of talking to her as if she were from the sticks or something. Maybe she should show up in some hideous gingham dress and embarrass him to death. "I do know a little about fashion, Chip," she said sweetly.

"Well, yes and no," Chip said.

"What's that supposed to mean?"

"It means you dress great," Chip told her, shooting her another toothpaste-ad smile.

"But when it comes to my parents, especially my mother, you might want to go easy on the flash."

Brittany arched an eyebrow. "The flash?"

"You know. Really short skirts and flashy colors. Don't get me wrong," he added with a wink, *"I think the way you dress is sexy. You just might want to tone it down a little for Saturday. First impressions, you know."*

"Shall I wear my hair in a bun?" Brittany asked acidly.

To her surprise, Chip actually seemed to be taking her suggestion seriously. "No, I don't think that's necessary," he said finally. "I know how girls feel about their hair. If you got it cut, say, to above your shoulders, you'd feel like you'd lost an arm, right?"

Brittany reached up and felt a strand of her long, glossy hair. Was Chip hinting? she wondered. First he wanted her to tone down the "flash," as he called it. Did he want her to chop her hair off, too?

Brittany clamped her lips together so she wouldn't start an argument. The only thing that really mattered to Chip were appearances, she knew. He was the editor of his school paper, but only because it would look great on his transcript for all those Ivy League college applications. Even Brittany, who cared about appearances as much as anyone, wrote for the *Record* because she really enjoyed it.

But if she wanted all the social prestige Chip Worthington could give her, then she'd have to put up with his terribly superior attitude.

"Oh, by the way," Chip said as he pulled up in front of River Heights High. "If you open the glove compartment, you'll find a little something in there for you."

Curious, Brittany pulled it open. The compartment was extremely neat, of course. Not a single wadded gum wrapper and no loose pieces of paper. Sitting on top of a perfectly folded map was a small box covered in dark blue velvet.

"Go ahead," Chip said, smiling at her questioning look. "Open it."

Brittany took the box out and snapped it open. Inside, nestled on a bed of pale blue satin, was a single strand of milky white pearls. The pearls had the barest hint of pink in them, like a blush. Brittany didn't have to ask if they were real. The Chip Worthingtons of this world didn't buy fake.

"Well?" Chip asked as she lifted the necklace out.

"Oh—Chip," Brittany said breathily.

"I thought you'd like pearls. Why don't

you wear them Saturday night?" he suggested. "They'd look really classy."

"They're beautiful," Brittany said. The pearls *were* gorgeous, but she had a very strange feeling as she undid the clasp to try them on. Maybe Chip hadn't given them to her to please *her*. He'd bought them to make sure she'd please his parents.

Brittany smiled at Chip, hoping she looked too overwhelmed with happiness to say anything. She'd known what she was getting into when she started dating Chip Worthington. She'd have to keep reminding herself of everything he could do for her. Otherwise, she might just haul off and slug him.

Inside the school Nikki had her eyes glued to Room 203. So far, nobody had done anything to make her suspicious. Nikki had no idea what she'd do if she *did* see anything fishy. Yell? Go to the principal? She wasn't sure. She just hoped, for Ellen's sake, that this would all be cleared up soon.

"Well, finally," Niles Butler said, coming up behind her. "I've been looking for you. I thought we were going to meet outside on the quad this morning."

"Oh, Niles, I forgot," Nikki said. "I'm sorry."

"That's all right." Niles reached out and

pushed a stray strand of Nikki's hair away from her eyes. "I hope you don't mind my asking, though, why you're leaning against this particular wall. Is it in danger of collapsing?"

Nikki laughed and shook her head. "I hope not," she said, trying to come up with a good reason for hanging out across from Room 203. "Actually, I'm just—I mean—well, I don't know. I thought it was a good place to stand," she finished lamely.

She wished she could tell Niles about Ellen's problem. She knew he wouldn't mention it to anyone else. But she couldn't. A promise was a promise.

Suddenly Nikki saw Kevin Hoffman coming down the hall. He came to a complete stop in front of Room 203, and Nikki held her breath as he felt in his back pocket. For his wallet, maybe? She let it out when Kevin didn't even glance at the door. She didn't know why he'd stopped, but he definitely wasn't going in. She didn't know whether to be disappointed or relieved.

Glancing up at Niles, she saw that he was watching Kevin, too, a curious look on his face. "Well," she said brightly, "I guess I'd better get to class. What about you?"

Niles's expression was quizzical, but he

didn't say anything. Oh, no, Nikki thought. There was no way to explain why she'd been staring at Kevin Hoffman. She hoped Niles didn't think she was interested in the guy. She loved Niles, and she was going to tell him so at dinner Saturday night.

"Pearls?" Kim Bishop stopped combing her long blond hair and stared at Brittany's reflection in the mirror of the girls' bathroom. "What are you asking about pearls for?"

Brittany dug in her bag and brought out the blue velvet box, which she opened.

"Nice," Kim commented, peering at the necklace. "My grandmother has one similar to it, except her clasp has diamonds."

Brittany snapped the box shut. "Chip gave it to me," she said, trying to forget Kim's remark about her grandmother.

Kim's blue eyes widened. "Well, well," she said. "He must really be interested if he's spending that kind of money. Why don't you look happier?"

Sighing, Brittany put the box back and told Kim about the dinner Saturday night with Chip's parents. "I think he bought them just so he'd be sure I'll look okay," she said. "He hinted around about getting my hair cut, and he practically came right out and told me to wear navy blue. 'Nothing too flashy' was the way he put it.''

"Well, you knew Chip was an incredible snob from the beginning," Kim pointed out. "I wouldn't care about that, of course, except that he's also a creep."

Brittany smothered a smile, remembering how Kim's boyfriend, Jeremy, had run away from Chip after losing badly at poker. The great Jeremy Pratt was still afraid of Chip, even though he'd never admit it. Not many people could outsnob Jeremy Pratt, but next to Chip he was Mr. Nice Guy.

"Well, anyway," Brittany said, "what do you think? About the pearls and the hair, I mean?" In spite of the fact that their boyfriends hated each other, she and Kim were still best friends. Kim understood exactly why Brittany was dating Chip, and she didn't make Brittany feel like a fraud.

"I don't know, Brittany," Kim said, picking a tiny piece of lint off her pink cashmere sweater. "It all depends on what you want. If you want to keep Chip, then you have to go along with him on this. If you don't want to go along with him, then . . ." Kim shrugged.

Brittany nodded. Kim didn't need to spell out what would happen if Brittany ignored Chip's hints about her clothes and hair and returned the pearls to him. He'd drop her so fast she wouldn't have time to blink.

Still breathless from gym class, Robin dashed around the corner and headed down the hall toward the student council room. Earlier, between classes, Nikki and Ellen had told her about Kevin Hoffman, but Robin had her doubts. Just because he knew how much they'd taken in from the tape and record sale didn't mean he'd stolen the money. A thief wouldn't stop to count how much there was; he'd just grab it. Come to think of it, why *had* the thief taken only part of the money? Why not all? Did he or she think it wouldn't be noticed?

Privately, Robin suspected Brittany Tate. Brittany had always dressed great, but lately, she'd been showing up in a new outfit every other day. Where was she getting the money for all those clothes?

When the bell rang, Robin ducked into the girls' bathroom until she was sure the hall would be clear. She had a free period now, and she usually spent it in the library. But she could catch up on her homework that night. It was more important to keep an eye out for any action around Room 203.

Pulling open the bathroom door, Robin peeked out. Good, the hall was empty. Trotting quietly in her sneakers, she walked to the end of the hall and around the corner a few feet. She couldn't be seen, but she'd be able to hear if anyone stopped at one of the doors.

Ten minutes later Robin heard footsteps. She'd been leaning against her locker, studying her English notes, but now she silently put her notebook on the floor and edged toward the corner.

The footsteps were still coming. Now they were slowing down. Robin inched closer to the corner and leaned her face against the wall. Then she slid her head around until she could see down the hallway with one eye.

"Hi!" someone shouted at her.

She pulled her head back in and held her breath. Maybe the person would turn back. No such luck, though. The footsteps continued, more rapidly now, straight for her.

**6**

"Hi, Robin!" Michael Quinn called, rounding the corner and catching Robin in her hiding place.

"Michael!" Robin stage-whispered. "Stop shouting my name. You're going to have every teacher in this wing coming out to see what's going on."

"Sorry," he said, lowering his voice. "What *is* going on, anyway?"

"I should be asking you that question," Robin told him. "I happen to have a free period, but what are you doing out of class?"

"Not class—band practice," Michael said. "I play trombone, in case you're interested. Anyway, practice was canceled. Everybody else stayed in the band room, but I felt like taking a walk. And I'm glad I did," he added, bouncing a little on the balls of his feet. He grinned. "Hey, I like that outfit."

Robin looked down at her blue shorts and blue- and white-striped T-shirt. "Michael, it's my gym uniform."

"Right. I knew that," Michael said quickly. "On you it looks great—that's what I meant."

Robin bit her lip to keep from laughing. "Well, anyway," she said, "don't let me keep you."

"Keep me?"

"From your walk," Robin reminded him.

"Oh, that." Stuffing his hands in the pockets of his jeans, Michael looked as if he planned to stick around for a long time. "To tell you the truth, I think I'm developing a blister on my left heel. As long as you're here, I'll just join you and give my foot a rest."

Robin sighed. Michael was kind of cute in a young sort of way, and she was flattered that he liked her so much, but she had a job to do.

While she was trying to think of a tactful way to tell him to scram, she heard another pair of footsteps. Grabbing Michael by a shirtsleeve, she pulled him flat against the lockers.

"Is this a game?" Michael asked. "Hide-and-seek, maybe?"

"Shhh!" Robin hissed. "Just stay here."

Again, she edged her way toward the corner and peered around it.

"Robin, hi!"

Robin felt as if she were in the middle of a TV sitcom. Now she was trapped by Calvin. So much for spying on the student council room, she thought.

"Robin, what are you doing here?" Calvin asked as he walked toward her. "I thought you'd be in the library."

Before Robin could come up with a good explanation, Michael's head popped around the corner. "Hide-and-seek, Cal," he said.

Calvin frowned at him and raised an eyebrow at Robin, who laughed. "We're not playing hide-and-seek," she told him. "I left the library to—um—get something from my locker. Michael's band practice was canceled, and we wound up in the same place."

"It was fate," Michael added.

"Right," Robin agreed.

Calvin looked at his watch. "Only fifteen more minutes until lunch," he said to Michael. "Sophomores eat early, right, Mike?"

Reluctantly, Michael nodded. "I guess I'll be on my way," he said. "See you at Platters later, right, Robin?"

"Sure, Michael. 'Bye." Robin waited until the red-haired boy was out of sight. Then she turned to Calvin. "How come you were so rude to him?" she asked.

Calvin shrugged. "The kid's crazy about you," he said. "And he bugs me."

"So what? Don't tell me you're jealous!" Robin couldn't believe it. "Cal, you know I don't care about Michael that way!"

"Yeah, but does *he* know?" Calvin asked.

"Well, if he doesn't, he must be blind," Robin said, putting her arm through Calvin's. "Anybody with halfway decent eyesight can see I'm crazy about you."

"Maybe you'd better tell him, anyway," Calvin said grumpily. "That kid just won't quit."

Later in the day, instead of using her free period to study, Ellen gathered some books and papers and made her way through the halls to the student council room. She'd talked to Nikki, and she'd suggested that Ellen should actually go into Room 203 and lock the door. If someone came, she could always hide in the closet.

Ellen knew she'd look like a total fool if somebody found her hiding in the closet, but she didn't care. She'd look much worse if everybody found out about the missing money.

As she stuck her key into the lock of the student council room, Ellen realized her hand was actually shaking. This is ridiculous, she told herself. Stop feeling guilty. You have every right to be here.

Ellen let herself into Room 203. Someone had shut the blinds against the afternoon sun, and the light was dim inside. Ellen flicked the light switch. That was when she noticed that the desk drawer was partially open.

Her heart pounding, Ellen moved quickly across the room and pulled the drawer all the way open. Inside was a single white envelope. And inside the envelope was a twenty-dollar bill.

"When could it have happened?" Nikki asked when Ellen told her about the money.

"Who knows?" Ellen said. "It's impossible to watch that room every hour of the day. Anyway, I didn't even bother to hide in the closet."

"No, I guess you wouldn't need to," Nikki agreed. "Whoever put that money there probably wouldn't do it twice in one day."

The bell rang, and the girls headed off in

opposite directions. As Ellen was hurrying down the hall toward her class, she noticed a poster on the wall. It was bright red, with the words "Watson, We Need You" in bold black letters covering almost the entire space. In smaller letters at the bottom, it said, "Vote for Alice Watson — Freshman Council."

Ellen stared at the poster for a minute, feeling rotten about not helping Suzanne with hers. She turned away quickly and bumped into Sasha Lopez, who was rushing down the hall in the opposite direction.

"Sorry, Sasha," Ellen murmured.

"It's okay," Sasha said. "I wasn't watching where I was going."

Sasha gave her a quick smile and started to move on, but Ellen stopped her.

"Sasha, could I ask you something?"

"Me?" Sasha said in surprise. She looked down the hallway. "Well, uh, sure."

"It'll only take a second. It's about that poster," Ellen said, pointing.

"Oh, the poster?" Sasha stepped back and looked at it. "Not bad. It doesn't say much about the girl, but maybe everybody already knows her. The color's eye-catching. Why?"

"My sister's running, too," Ellen explained. "But she's very shy, and most of the kids probably don't know her like they know this Alice Watson. You're really good at this kind of thing," she went on. "What kind of poster do you think would be right for her?"

"Oh, Ellen, I'm not sure," Sasha said. "I mean, I'll try to think about it, okay?" She glanced down the hall. "I really have to hurry now."

"Right," Ellen said. "Go ahead, Sasha. Maybe we can talk another time."

Sighing, Ellen watched Sasha hurry down the hall, her short hair sticking up like the quills on a porcupine. She was disappointed, but she shouldn't have expected Sasha to come up with a brilliant idea on the spot. It would have been nice, though. Then she could have told Suzanne, and she'd have had one less thing to feel guilty about.

When the final bell rang, Nikki headed for her locker, trying to decide whether to stake out the student council room that afternoon. As she'd told Ellen, the chances that the thief would put money back two times in one day seemed awfully slim. And Niles had asked her to go for pizza after school, which she really wanted to do. She'd put him off, though, and said she wasn't sure she could.

At her locker, Nikki checked her hair in the little mirror she'd taped inside. What a mess! It looked as if she hadn't combed it all day.

Rummaging in her bag, Nikki found a small brush and got to work. While she was struggling with a bad tangle, she saw a pair of gray eyes reflected in her mirror.

"Hi, Nikki," Tim Cooper said.

Nikki caught her breath and turned around to smile at him. She and Tim had gone together for a while at the beginning of the year. Nikki had felt awful when they broke up, but now, with Niles in her life, the hurt was gone.

"How's it going?" Tim asked casually.

"Fine. Great, actually," Nikki said. "How about you?"

"Not bad."

Not the most enthusiastic answer, Nikki thought. Tim looked as good as ever, but she couldn't help wondering just how happy he was.

"Well," Tim said, "I guess I'll be going. You look good, Nikki," he added.

"Not yet, but I'm trying." Nikki laughed, waving her brush in the air. "But thanks, anyway."

Turning to go, Tim narrowly missed bumping into Niles, who'd just walked up. "Excuse me," Tim said, swerving around Niles. "Good to see you, Nikki."

"You, too." Nikki gave her hair another quick once-over and stuffed the brush back into her bag. "Hi," she said to Niles. "Don't tell me—let me guess. You're starving and only pizza will do."

"Only pizza with *you* will do," Niles corrected her, smiling.

"Well . . ." Nikki shut her locker door. She had to say no. She just couldn't let Ellen down, no matter how much she'd rather be with Niles. "I guess you're going to have to starve, then," she said lightly.

Niles looked disappointed. "You can't go?"

"I'm afraid not," Nikki said. "I really want to, Niles, but I promised to do a favor for a friend, and I'm already late." She hoped he wouldn't ask what friend or what favor. She wasn't good at making things up on the spot.

But Niles was much too polite to pry. "I suppose I'll just have to curb my insane craving for pizza, then," he said. His eyes followed Tim Cooper down the hall.

First Kevin Hoffman and now Tim, Nikki thought. Niles must think I'm losing interest in him. Nothing was further from the truth. She loved Niles, but she couldn't tell him now. She had to get to the student council room. Besides, she needed the rest of the week until Saturday night to work up the courage to come right out and say it.

"Niles, listen," she said. "There's something I want to tell you, but I can't right now."

"Oh?" Niles looked a little worried. "Is it important?"

"Yes, very important," Nikki said, blushing.

"But you can't tell me now?"

Nikki shook her head.

"Complicated, is it?"

"Yes and no," Nikki said.

"Don't leave me in suspense. Give me a hint at least," Niles pleaded. "Is it good or bad?"

"Oh, it's good!" Nikki assured him quickly. "I mean, I think it's good."

"Nikki—"

"Niles, I can't." Nikki laughed, embarrassed that she'd even started this. "I really have to go now, but I'll tell you Saturday night."

"Saturday? But this is Wednesday," Niles protested. "You're going to keep me waiting three days?"

Nikki stretched up and kissed him quickly. "I've got to run," she said. "Don't worry, the news will keep."

With that, Nikki raced off down the hall, leaving a mystified Niles staring after her.

\* \* \*

Later that afternoon, Ellen and Nikki met Nancy Drew at a coffee shop in town to bring her up to date on what was happening. Nancy listened without saying a thing, her concentration complete.

"So we're just going to keep watching the room," Nikki finished. "It's really the only thing we can do."

Nancy nodded and tucked her reddish blond hair behind her ears. "You're right," she agreed. "If you start asking questions, then people will know the money's missing."

"And I can't let that happen," Ellen said, stirring her soda with a straw. "I might have to say something soon, I know. But I'm not ready to give up yet."

"I understand." Nancy gave her an encouraging smile. "But listen, the fact that somebody's putting the money back is really great. Whoever it is must be feeling awfully guilty to take a risk like that. And it gives you a much better chance of finding out who did it."

"I know," Ellen said with a sigh. "But I almost don't care who did it anymore. I just wish they'd put it all back so the whole thing would be over."

"I don't blame you," Nikki told her. "I'm actually a little afraid to find out who it is. I mean, what if it's somebody I know?"

"It probably is," Nancy said, stirring her coffee. "But you can't let that keep you from trying to catch her. Or him. You're doing the right thing by staking out the student council room," she added. "Just keep it up. One of these days, you and the thief will be there at the same time."

## 7

"Psst! Robin!"

Startled, Robin looked up from the pile of CDs she was pricing at Platters. Michael was peering over her shoulder.

"Don't look now, but I think you've marked those wrong," he said.

"I couldn't have!" Quickly Robin flipped through the pages of the pricing sheet Lenny had given her. "There," she said, pointing to the paper. " 'Electric Heat—sixteen dollars and ninety-five cents.' That's the green sticker, see?"

"That was last week," Michael said, pointing to the date. "This week, electric Heat goes back up to eighteen dollars and ninety-five cents. The blue sticker."

"Let me see that." Frowning, Robin bent her head closer to the paper, and her earrings —bright orange stars dangling from a silver half-moon—swung against her cheeks.

"I really like the earrings you wear," Michael commented, his head close to hers. "I like everything you wear, as a matter of fact."

"Thanks, Michael," Robin murmured, still studying the pricing sheet.

"Take that outfit," Michael went on. "I mean, how many girls could wear a yellow man's shirt and chartreuse knee pants and look fantastic? That's the color, isn't it?" he asked. "Chartreuse?"

"Oh, no, it *is* blue!" Robin cried.

"The pants?"

"What? No, the CD sticker," Robin said, confused. "What do my pants have to do with this?"

"Nothing," Michael said, blushing a little. "I was just admiring your outfit, that's all."

"Oh. Well, thanks. But now what am I going to do?" Robin moaned, checking her watch. "Lenny had to go to the bank, but he'll be back any minute. He's absolutely going to freak when he sees this!"

"I'll help you," Michael said eagerly.

"I thought you had to unload that new shipment of tapes," Robin told him.

"Done," Michael said triumphantly.

"Already? That was fast."

"Fast is my middle name." With a shy grin, Michael picked up a sheet of blue stickers. "Come on. We'll make a great team."

Robin patted him on the shoulder. "Michael," she said, "what did I ever do without you?"

Down the hall from Platters, Brittany pulled open the door of a shop called Très Chic. She'd never shopped there before because the clothes in the window were usually the kind of stuff her mother wore—elegant but plain.

Don't think of them as plain, Brittany told herself as she moved across the deep white carpeting toward a rack of dresses. They're simple. Understated. Chic.

Reluctantly bypassing a two-piece outfit in red silk that immediately caught her eye, Brittany moved along the rack until she came to a dress made of some kind of soft, dark green material. Padded shoulders and a low, scooped-out back saved it from being totally boring. It might just do, Brittany thought.

"That just arrived today," a saleswoman said, gliding up beside Brittany. "Lovely, isn't it?"

"Lovely," Brittany echoed, searching for a price tag. Where was the stupid thing, anyway? "Could you tell me—"

"Four-fifty."

Brittany could feel the blood drain from her face. Four hundred and fifty dollars! On second thought, this was not the kind of dress her mother would wear. Her mother couldn't afford to spend that kind of money on a single dress. Who could—except somebody like Mrs. Worthington? Four hundred and fifty dollars was probably small change to her.

"Would you like to try it on?" the saleswoman asked.

Brittany pretended to think about it. "Actually, no," she said as casually as possible. "It's beautiful, but it just isn't me."

Before the woman could make any suggestions about other dresses, Brittany thanked her and left the store. She'd been crazy to go in there, anyway. Très Chic was not *très* cheap—and cheap was the only way she could go.

By the time Lenny Lukowski returned from the bank, Robin and Michael had finished covering up the green stickers with blue ones, and the Electric Heat CDs were all in place.

"Hey, nice work, Robin," Lenny commented, checking out the CDs.

"You sound surprised, Lenny," Robin said. She winked at Michael. "I'm insulted."

"Come on, Robin. You know you've messed up more than a few times."

"Not this time," Michael said quickly. "Things went smooth as silk. Plus," he added, "the new tapes that came in are all unpacked, the stockroom's swept, we did forty-three dollars' worth of business, and Robin called in the ad for next week's sale. Personally, I think we both deserve a raise."

"You wish," Lenny grumbled as he headed back toward the office. At the door, he stopped. "Take a coffee break instead," he suggested. "It's my best offer."

After Lenny had disappeared into the office, Robin burst out laughing. "Michael," she said, throwing an arm around his shoulder, "you're terrific!"

At that moment, the bell over the door jangled, and Calvin Roth walked in.

Half an hour after leaving Très Chic, Brittany stood in the dressing room of Debs, another store she hardly ever went into because it was so preppy. She'd bought a couple of sweaters there, though, and at least she knew the prices wouldn't make her faint.

Zipping up the dress she'd picked out, she stepped back and surveyed herself in the mirror.

The dress was simple—a soft burgundy material that looked like wool but was less expensive. It had a slightly scooped neck, long, close-fitting sleeves, and a flared skirt that hit her just below the knees.

All she needed were Chip's pearls and a pair of low-heeled sensible shoes, and she'd look at least thirty, Brittany thought in disgust. Maybe that was Chip's point.

The price was right, though. She could buy this dress without having to waitress again at Slim & Shorty's Good Eats Cafe. Brittany knew she'd rather hock the pearl necklace and tell Chip she'd lost it before ever setting foot in that greasy spoon again.

Sighing, Brittany checked her reflection again. It wasn't the worst dress in the world, she decided. And it wouldn't kill her to wear it one time.

But sensible shoes were definitely out. She had a pair with high, ultrathin heels, and they'd go perfectly with the dress. She had to wear *something* she liked. If Chip disapproved, then she just might strangle him with his striped Talbot tie.

* * *

"Hey, how come you're so quiet?" Robin asked as Calvin drove her home after work. "You haven't said two words since we left the mall. Not that you're normally a chatterbox," she teased, "but you usually talk more than this."

"I just don't feel like talking, I guess," Calvin said, and shrugged. "Anyway, I thought you'd be sick of talk after listening to Mike yammer all afternoon."

Robin stretched out her long, slender legs as far as she could and leaned her head back against the seat. "I get it," she said. "You're mad because you thought I was hugging Michael. It wasn't really a hug, you know."

"You could have fooled me." Cal's expression was grim.

"Oh, come on, Cal." Robin gave him a little punch on the arm. "I told you what happened. I told you how he saved me by helping with all those stickers."

"Right. And then he told Lenny how fantastic you are," Calvin added.

"It was funny!" Robin cried. "It's his second day on the job and he's already asking for a raise! I just put my arm around his shoulder, like he was a little brother or something."

"It didn't look all that sisterly to me,"

Calvin said. "He wasn't looking at you the way a brother would, either. You should have seen him—like a lovesick calf. It was disgusting."

"I always wondered about that expression," Robin said with a giggle. "Do calves really get lovesick?"

"Like a puppy who got a pat on the head, then," Calvin said, exasperated. "You know what I mean."

"Okay, okay." Robin bit back another giggle and tried to look serious. "I understand what you're saying, but, Calvin, I really think you're exaggerating. Michael has a crush on me—okay, I agree. And I admit, I'm a little flattered. But he knows you're my boyfriend, and pretty soon he'll give up."

"Don't count on it," Calvin warned. "Next thing you know, he'll be walking by your house, just so he can feel close to you."

Before Robin had a chance to answer, Calvin brought the car to a screeching halt. "If you think I'm crazy," he said, "just take a look."

Robin sat up and squinted through the windshield in the direction Calvin was pointing. Sure enough, way down at the end of the street, right in front of her house, was a figure pedaling along on a black mountain bike. It was early evening, and just beginning to get dark, but she could see enough of the red hair to tell that it was Michael Quinn.

After stashing her new dress in her mother's flower shop, Brittany walked a few feet down the hall, took a very deep breath, and pushed open the door of the Clip Shop.

A girl with thickly moussed hair glanced up from the curved front desk. "Yes?"

"I'd like a—a haircut," Brittany said faintly, wondering if she could really go through with it.

"Sure." The girl spun around on her high stool and gestured at one of the hairstylists, a girl whose short hair stood up in inch-long spikes.

Before she had time for any second thoughts, Brittany was whisked to a small room at the back and draped in a soft black cover to protect her clothes. Then her long hair was washed, conditioned, and rinsed.

With a towel around her wet hair, Brittany followed the spiky-haired girl, who'd introduced herself as Liz, to a chair in the large mirrored styling room.

"How much do you want me to take off?" Liz asked as she combed out Brittany's wet hair.

"Well, I think maybe just a trim," Brittany said. "Enough to get it a little above my shoulders."

Liz took a clump of hair and twisted it up, fastening it on top of Brittany's head with a big clip. "That's a lot more than a trim," she said. "To get it to your shoulders, I'll have to take off a couple of inches."

Brittany cringed. She'd spent years growing her hair to this length. Could she stand to have even a few precious inches hacked off just to please that jerk Chip Worthington?

By now, most of her hair was twisted up in clips. Liz had left two hunks in the front hanging down on either side of her face. Taking hold of one of the clumps, Liz pointed with her scissors. "That's three inches," she said. "But I'll start lower, and you tell me when to stop."

Brittany stared at herself in the mirror for a long moment. Then with a gulp, she said, "Okay. Go ahead."

 **8**

When Ellen's alarm buzzed Thursday morning, she quickly shut it off and pulled the pillow over her head. She didn't want to get up and get dressed. She didn't want to go to school and stake out the student council room. She didn't want to try to avoid Ms. Rose. All she wanted to do was stay buried under the covers and forget about the missing money.

But she couldn't forget, no matter how hard she tried. It was the last thing on her mind before she went to sleep and the first thing she thought of when she woke up.

She couldn't hide in bed forever, either. Maybe she could pretend to be sick for one day, but when she went back the next day, the problem would still be waiting for her. She might as well get up and face it now.

Dragging herself out of bed, Ellen pulled on her fuzzy green bathrobe and walked slowly down the hall to the bathroom. After washing up, she walked just as slowly down the stairs and into the kitchen.

"Good morning," her mother said, raising her eyes from the newspaper. "Is Suzanne up yet?"

"I guess so," Ellen said with a yawn. She opened the refrigerator and took out the carton of orange juice. "I heard her radio when I went by her room."

Pouring herself a glass of juice, Ellen sat down at the table across from her mother.

"No breakfast?" Mrs. Ming asked. "Not even toast?"

Ellen shook her head. "I'm not very hungry, Mom." She took a sip of juice, even though she didn't want that, either.

Mrs. Ming studied her for a moment. "Ellen," she said, "I don't mean to pry, but I have to ask. Is something wrong, honey?"

"What do you mean?" Ellen asked.

"Well, you have seemed very quiet lately," her mother said. "But mainly, I'm concerned about the way you're treating Suzanne."

"I don't understand," Ellen said, even though she understood perfectly.

"Running for the freshman council is a very big thing to your sister," Mrs. Ming said. "She's scared to death and she needs a lot of support. She hasn't come right out and told me, but I know she's disappointed that you haven't been more supportive."

"I told her I thought it was great," Ellen said defensively. "And I do. But I'm really busy, Mom. I can't run her campaign for her."

"She doesn't expect that," Mrs. Ming said, getting up and rinsing out her coffee cup. "But you can't be too busy to ask her how things are going, can you? Tell her you think she has a good chance? Show her you're on her side?"

"No," Ellen murmured. "I'm not too busy for that."

"Good." Mrs. Ming patted Ellen's shoulder and left the kitchen to finish dressing for work.

Ellen poured the rest of her juice down the sink and went up to Suzanne's room. She could still hear the radio, and she had to knock loudly before Suzanne pulled the door open.

"Hi," Ellen said, stepping into the room.

"Listen, I talked to Sasha Lopez yesterday about ideas for your poster. She said she'd try to think of something."

"Oh. Well, thanks, but it's a little late now." Suzanne turned away and walked over to her bed. She picked up a large sheet of paper and held it out. "I did four of these last night," she said. "It's not nearly enough, but at least I'll have something up to compete with Alice Watson. I'll do more tonight."

Ellen looked at the poster and her heart sank. It was simple, all right, just the way Suzanne wanted. White paper with black lettering that said, "Vote for Suzanne Ming —Freshman Council."

Suzanne was in a hurry to get something up in the school halls, but next to Alice Watson's bright red posters, these wouldn't get a second glance, Ellen knew.

She cleared her throat. "I'll try to help you do more of them," she said. "Maybe tonight or over the weekend."

Suzanne shrugged. "It doesn't matter," she said, not looking at her sister. "I don't really have a chance of winning, anyway."

Robin loved her early-morning workouts in the high-school pool. It was a quarter to eight, and she'd already done twenty laps. As she reached the end of the lane, she executed a smooth racing turn, pushed herself off with a powerful kick of her legs, and headed back for the other end. She'd get in ten more laps and then call it quits.

Just as she was about to make another turn, Robin saw a pair of sneakered feet standing at the edge of the pool. She didn't even need to look any farther to know that they must belong to Michael.

She pulled herself over to the edge and raised her eyes up at him, blinking the water away.

"Hi!" he said. "I just happened to be walking by."

Sure, Robin thought.

"Don't let me interrupt," Michael went on. "I know how important your training is. I'll just watch."

Robin pulled herself out of the pool and stood next to him, water dripping off her sleek tank suit. "I was just about finished, anyway," she said, gasping a little. She peeled off her cap and shook her hair.

"I hope you don't mind an extremely unoriginal observation," Michael said, "but you're like a fish in the water."

"Out of the water, too," Robin said with a laugh. "According to Lenny, anyway."

"Lenny just doesn't appreciate you." Michael's gray eyes gazed at her admiringly.

Robin grabbed her towel and wrapped it around herself. It was a good thing Calvin wasn't there, she thought. She really couldn't understand why this whole thing bothered him so much, though. He kept saying he wasn't jealous, but he sure was acting like it.

"So!" Michael said hopefully. "If you're done, why don't I hang around and wait while you get changed? I could walk you to class."

"That would be really out of your way, wouldn't it?" Robin asked, drying her face. "You're way over in the other wing."

"Yeah, I guess so." Michael stepped back directly into a large puddle of water. Even though he was wearing sneakers, he almost slipped on the wet tiles. "Well, okay. How about if you let me buy you a soda on our coffee break this afternoon?"

"We can't take a break at the same time," Robin reminded him gently. He was so cute, she thought, and so nice, she really didn't want to hurt his feelings. Did Cal really expect her to tell him to get lost?

"You're right about that, too." Michael grinned at her and shuffled his feet a little, splashing water on his jeans.

"Well, listen, I'd better change," Robin

said, starting to move away. "But I'll see you later at work, okay?"

"Uh, Robin?"

She stopped and turned back. Michael hadn't moved.

"I lied," he said.

"You lied?" Robin repeated, puzzled.

"About walking by here," he admitted, his face getting red. "Actually, I had an ulterior motive." He took a deep breath. "The real reason I came by was to ask you if you might want to go biking with me sometime, or to a movie." He held up his hand. "Don't answer now," he said quickly. "Think about it awhile—take as long as you want. I'm an A student, I play a mean trombone, I'm not a bad swimmer, and I think we'd have a good time. I can't drive yet," he added, "but, hey, nobody's perfect, right?"

Michael had been backing away the whole time he was talking, and now he was at the door. With a little lopsided grin, he turned and left the pool room.

Uh-oh, Robin thought. A crush was one thing, but actually asking her out was something else. She knew she'd say no, of course. But first she had to figure out how to do it without hurting his feelings. She also knew she wasn't going to tell Calvin about it. She hated keeping secrets from him, but he was so touchy about the whole subject, he'd never understand. And what he didn't know wouldn't hurt him, would it?

Out on the quad, Nikki was standing alone, searching for Niles. He'd said he might be a little late, but she hoped he'd come soon. She wanted to see him before she had to run in and stand guard outside the student council room. If he had to come looking for her again, he was really going to think something weird was going on.

Glancing around the crowded quad, Nikki spotted Robin hurrying toward her. It was very cold that morning, and Robin was wearing a hat, which she rarely did. Of course, Robin wouldn't wear just any hat, Nikki thought with a smile. This morning, it was a Day-Glo orange stocking cap with a huge tassle on the end.

"Hi," Robin called, hurrying over to Nikki. "Have you seen Cal or Lacey?"

"No, not yet."

"You're never going to believe what happened," Robin said. "Michael asked me out!"

"That cute sophomore?" Nikki asked. "That's really nice."

"Yeah, it was," Robin agreed. "Not that I'm going, of course."

"So what does Calvin think about all this?" Nikki asked.

"That's why I'm glad he's not around," Robin told her. "He'd be furious. He's gotten all jealous about Michael, and it's starting to make me mad."

"Calvin? He doesn't seem like the jealous type to me, Robin," Nikki said. "Especially when he has to know you're crazy about him."

"That's what I told him," Robin said. "I'm starting to think I don't understand guys very well."

"Talk to him about it," Nikki suggested. "Maybe he just needs to hear you say you love him."

"Maybe I will," Robin agreed. "But I'll have to find a locked room to do it in. Otherwise Michael will find us and interrupt." She laughed. "He has this habit of turning up wherever I am."

Nikki laughed, too, but when she caught sight of Ellen Ming, she stopped. Ellen had just come out of the school building. She was standing on the steps, turning her head right and left almost frantically. When she spotted Nikki and Robin she ran toward them.

"Something must have happened," Nikki said.

"Yeah, she looks pretty excited," Robin agreed. "Maybe she caught the thief."

Both girls hurried to meet Ellen in the middle of the quad.

"What is it?" Nikki asked. "Good news or bad?"

"Good, I guess," Ellen said a little breathlessly. She glanced around and lowered her voice. "More money," she whispered. "Another twenty dollars."

"You're kidding," Robin said. "When did you find it?"

"Just a minute ago," Ellen told her. "I'd been waiting outside the student council room ever since the building opened this morning. Nobody went in. Nobody came out. Anyway," she continued, "I was just about to leave when I remembered that I'd left the bankbook in there."

"I thought you took it home," Nikki said.

"That was the ledger," Ellen explained. "I don't know why I left the bankbook. I guess I just haven't been thinking straight lately."

"So you went in to get it and you found another twenty dollars?" Robin asked.

Ellen nodded. "And I don't know when it was put there," she said. "Believe me, I watched that room like a hawk."

"I think I know," Nikki said guiltily. "It must have happened yesterday after school. I ran into Tim at my locker, and then Niles and I talked for a few minutes—" She broke off and sighed. "It was my fault. If I'd just gone there the minute classes were over, I might have seen something."

"Don't blame yourself, Nikki," Ellen told her. "We can't watch the room every second of the day."

"Ellen's right," Robin said. "But I think we should try a little harder if we can. This makes the third time the thief has put money back. And the second time in two days."

"That's why I guess it's good news," Ellen agreed. "Somebody's trying to pay it all back, I think. So they're going to keep on doing it." She tucked her hair behind her ears and smiled grimly. "I don't think it'll be very long before we know exactly who our mystery person is."

# 9 ～～

Like Robin, Brittany was wearing a hat that morning, too—but not because of the cold and not because her hair was wet. Wet hair would have been fine with Brittany. Even dirty hair would have been an improvement over what was underneath her plum-colored knit hat.

Glancing furtively around the quad, Brittany hurried up the steps and straight into the school building. So far, so good. What she wanted to do was get to the nearest girls' room without running into anyone she knew. She'd overslept and there hadn't been time to do anything but grab the nearest hat. But maybe the damage wasn't so bad as it had looked in her mirror earlier. Maybe she'd just been having a bad dream.

Good, the girls' room was empty. Plopping her books on the shelf above the sinks, Brittany stepped back, took a deep breath, and pulled off the hat.

"Brittany! What happened?"

"What did you do to yourself?"

Brittany tried to get the hat back on, but it was too late. Kim and Samantha had come in too fast. Now they were standing behind her, gaping at her as if she'd suddenly grown a second head.

Samantha recovered her voice first. "My, my," she said in her lilting southern accent, "you've really gone and done it now, haven't you?"

"Is it that bad?" Brittany whispered.

Kim narrowed her eyes and stared at Brittany's hair, considering. "It's not a complete disaster," she decided. "Not quite, anyway."

Brittany turned back to the mirror. Maybe it wasn't a total disaster, but it came close. The back of her hair was still long. So was the left side. But the entire right side was a full two inches shorter.

"I take it that's not the latest style," Kim remarked. "So what happened?"

"I panicked," Brittany said. She explained to Samantha about the upcoming dinner ordeal, and Chip's suggestion that she get her hair cut. "So there I was in the Clip Shop," she went on. "I told the girl to go ahead and cut it, but after she'd made the first cut, I realized I couldn't go through with it. I told her to stop. Then I paid the full price and ran out of there with my head still full of those gigantic clips! I think they thought I was crazy."

Samantha couldn't help smiling. "You must have been quite a sight," she commented.

"Maybe you ought to go back and get the rest of it cut," Kim said. "Or at least the other side. Then it wouldn't look lopsided."

"I can't go back there," Brittany wailed.

"Then go someplace else," Samantha suggested. "Or cut it yourself."

"I guess I could do that," Brittany agreed with a sigh. "This isn't even the worst of it—well, I guess it is. I had to buy a dress I'll probably never wear again in my life, and I have to wear Chip's stupid pearl necklace, and . . ."

"All this for the Worthingtons?" Samantha asked.

"Well, I want them to like me," Brittany

said quickly. "I just don't want to get my hair cut, that's all."

"Seems like you're doing an awful lot of things you hate just to please Chip the Creep," Kim said. "Personally, I'd tell him to get lost."

Well, you can afford to, Brittany thought. *I* can't. "Chip's probably just nervous about Saturday night," she said. "After I meet his parents and everything goes smoothly, he'll stop worrying. So all I have to do is make a good impression on them, and everything will be fine." She picked up the short half of her hair and tucked it behind her ear.

"That doesn't work," Kim said bluntly. "Push both sides back. Or wear it up and try to twist that piece into it."

"Here." Samantha took two blue enameled clips out of her own cinnamon-colored hair and handed them to Brittany. "These'll help for today and, anyway, Kyle prefers my hair down, not pulled back." Kyle Kirkwood was Samantha's latest conquest and cause. She had changed him from geek to gorgeous with the right clothes and haircut in a few short weeks.

"Thanks," Brittany said gratefully. Using the hair clips, she anchored both sides of her hair behind her ears. She wasn't crazy about the style, but she guessed it would do for one day. It still looked off balance, though. She'd have to do something before Saturday night.

Staring at herself glumly in the mirror, Brittany realized she just might wind up wearing her hair in a bun after all.

"See anything?" Ellen asked Nikki as she came to relieve her on duty between classes later that day.

"No mystery person," Nikki said. "But Ms. Rose was in and out of the room a couple of times."

"I was afraid of that," Ellen said. "I told her I'd have the ledger book up to date by next week's meeting. She's probably hoping I got it done early." She glanced up and down the hall. "I hope she doesn't come by while I'm here. I hate lying."

"You haven't really lied," Nikki assured her. "Besides, maybe we'll get lucky and have this thing solved by next week."

"I hope so," Ellen said. "Anyway, go ahead and get to class, Nikki. It won't matter if I'm a little bit late."

After Nikki left, Ellen leaned back against the lockers and took out her French book.

She'd had been studying for a couple of minutes when she heard someone coming.

Looking up, she saw Kevin Hoffman hurrying down the hall toward her. Her heart began to pound. She buried her face in her French book, but it didn't do any good, naturally.

"Ellen!" Kevin called. "Fancy meeting you here."

You, too, Ellen thought. "Hi, Kevin," she said.

"This must be my lucky day," Kevin said. "Ben asked me to get something from the student council room, and guess what? On my way here, I remembered that I lost my key."

"Oh?"

"I just noticed it was missing the other day," he went on. "No telling how long it's been gone. Promise you won't rat on me to Ms. Rose?" he added with a grin. "She doesn't really consider me student council material. This would give her a good excuse to come down on me."

"I won't tell," Ellen said. Had he really lost his key? she wondered, then instantly hated herself for suspecting him. She tried to smile sweetly at him. After this was all over, she really hoped to start seeing him.

"I knew I could count on you," Kevin told her. "Anyway, like I said, it's my lucky day.

You've got a key, right?" he asked. "So you can let me in."

"Sure." Taking her key out of her bag, Ellen went over to Room 203 and unlocked it. The two of them went in together, and Kevin headed straight for the big closet.

"Hey, I saw your sister's running for freshman council," he said, rummaging through some papers.

"Mm-hmm."

"Carrying on the tradition, right?"

"What tradition?" Ellen asked.

Kevin pulled his head out of the closet. "You know, running for office," he said. "Service to the school, stuff like that."

"Oh." Ellen shrugged. "Yes, I guess she is."

"Ah-ha! Here it is." Kevin took out a stack of stationery. "Ben wants us to write a bunch of thank-yous to the businesses that supported the school cleanup campaign," he explained.

"That's a good idea," Ellen said.

"Well, you thought of the cleanup," Kevin told her. "Maybe I should write *you* a thank-you letter, too." After another quick grin and a hand gently placed on her shoulder, Kevin hurried out of the room.

Ellen left more slowly, making sure the door was locked. Kevin didn't act as if he had anything to hide, she thought. Why did she have any doubts about him at all?

If Kevin really *had* lost his key, then whoever stole the money must be using it to get into the student-council room. She could hardly go around checking people's lockers and purses and pockets. If only there was a way to ask without being obvious about it.

Still, it was a lead. Maybe not a big one, but enough to make Ellen think they might just crack this case after all.

At Platters that afternoon Robin tried desperately to avoid Michael. Of course they were working in the same store, but Lenny had put Michael in charge of the customers and he'd sent Robin into the stockroom to unpack new merchandise. The store was busy and Robin figured that Michael wouldn't have time to stand around and admire her outfit or tell her how great she was.

But somehow, Michael kept finding the time. His first excuse was that one of the customers wanted an LP she was unpacking.

"Here you go," Robin said, handing him the record.

"Thanks." Michael took it but didn't leave right away. "By the way," he said, "I saw this wild pair of earrings at that booth downstairs—silver, in the shape of lightning bolts. And I said to myself, 'Those are definitely Robin.' "

"Michael!" Lenny's voice called from the front of the store. "Customers are backing up out here!"

Reluctantly, Michael left the storeroom, but he was back again in fifteen minutes. "Lenny really exaggerates," he said. "There were only two customers."

"Well, you'd better not hang out here very long," Robin told him. "My time in this place is almost up, but you just started. You don't want to lose your job the first week."

Michael's face fell. "You mean you're quitting?"

"Not exactly," Robin said. "Didn't I tell you this is only temporary employment for me?"

Michael shook his head.

"Oh. Well, I'm just taking my friend Lacey's place here until she can come back," Robin explained. "And Lacey will be starting again next week." Thank heavens, she added to herself.

Michael stared at his feet for a few seconds. Then he smiled. "Well, we'll still see each other a lot at school, right? And I bet you come by here a lot to see your friend."

"Not that often," Robin told him gently.

"And we're in different grades, remember? We really won't be running into each other that much."

Before Michael could answer, Lenny shouted for him again and he had to leave.

There, Robin thought. She'd practically come right out and told Michael that they wouldn't be spending *any* time together after she finished at Platters. He was smart—he'd take the hint. It ought to satisfy Calvin, too, in case he asked.

When Michael didn't come back to the stockroom again, Robin was sure he'd understood. Then she started to worry that she'd hurt his feelings. Sometimes, she wasn't the most subtle person in the world.

As soon as she'd finished putting a bunch of tapes on one of the stockroom shelves, Robin went out into the store. She had to make sure Michael wasn't pining away or anything.

She found him by the front window, putting stickers on CDs. He certainly didn't seem to be heartbroken. In fact, he looked totally cheerful.

"Hi," she said. "Where's Lenny?"

"He stepped out to get a cup of coffee," Michael told her. "I gave him some money and asked him to buy us something, too. Soda for me, juice for you."

"Thanks, but why juice?" Robin asked.

"Well, I figured that with your swimming and everything, you didn't drink much soda," Michael said. Suddenly he looked worried. "Was I wrong? I mean, you can have my soda. Juice is fine with me. Or, hey, I'll go find Lenny and change the order."

"Michael, it's okay!" Robin said. She waved one arm in the air, knocking the precariously stacked pile of CDs to the floor.

Immediately they both knelt down to pick them up.

"This reminds me of how we met," Michael said.

Robin grinned at him. "No, we met over a bunch of tapes," she said. "But you're right, I was the one who dropped them."

Their heads were almost touching as they bent over the pile of CDs. Robin was smiling at Michael, and Michael had a silly grin on his face, staring at her as if he'd never seen anyone so fantastic in his life.

Robin had a creepy feeling that she was being observed. Slowly she lifted her eyes to the front window. Standing there peering in at her and Michael was Calvin.

# 10

As Calvin walked into Platters, Robin heard the buzzer sound over the door. "Cal, hi!" Scooping up some more tapes, she dumped them on the shelf inside the window and stood up. "You're early," she said, moving over to greet him.

"Just twenty minutes," Calvin muttered, two spots of red high on his cheeks.

Michael stood up, too. "Good to see you, Cal," he said.

"Mmmm," Calvin managed to say through gritted teeth.

Calvin was looking super grim, Robin thought. It was obvious that he was still ridiculously jealous of Michael Quinn.

"Well!" she said brightly to Calvin.

"Lenny's really taking his time getting that coffee. When he gets back it'll almost be time to go. You know what I'm dying for? A double-thick milk shake from Sundae's Child. Chocolate."

"Sounds great!" Michael said eagerly as if he'd been invited.

Calvin shot him a nasty look. "Don't you have homework or something?"

"As a matter of fact, I do," Michael said cheerfully. "But I can spare a little time."

"Well, I can't." Turning to Robin, Calvin said, "I'll meet you outside, okay?"

Robin nodded, frowning as she watched him leave the store. She was getting a little tired of this jealousy bit. Why couldn't he lighten up?

After school Brittany was sitting in front of her dressing table, trying to come up with a decent way to camouflage the damage to her hair.

When her bedside phone rang, Brittany hurried over and picked up the receiver. She was happy to forget about her hair for the moment. "Hello?"

"Hi."

"Hello, Chip." Chip never identified himself, but the confidence in his voice was unmistakable.

"There's been a change in plans for Saturday," he said.

Brittany lowered herself onto the bed. "You mean it's off?" she asked, trying not to sound too hopeful.

"No, nothing like that," Chip told her. "But my parents already made plans to see some friends before dinner, so they won't be going to the club with us. We'll meet them there."

"Oh, well, that's fine." Brittany was just as glad she wouldn't be riding in the car with them. She'd have extra time to think of clever conversation before she met them at the club.

"So," Chip said. "Are you all set?"

Brittany lifted the short half of her hair and looked across the room at her reflection. "Not yet, but I will be," she said sweetly. Maybe if she wore an extralong earring on that side, it would all balance out.

"Good," Chip said. "Listen, I know you're probably nervous."

Well, of course I'm nervous, Brittany wanted to yell. Who wouldn't be, the way Chip kept making such a big deal about it? "Maybe a little," she said lightly.

"I thought so," he said. "Listen, don't bother trying to think of things to talk about. My father just bought a new yacht, so you can discuss that with him. My mother does all kinds of charity work, and she's really into roses." He chuckled. "That ought to get you through the main course, right?"

"Probably even through dessert," Brittany told him. She didn't know the first thing about yachts, but roses she could manage, thanks to her mother.

"Okay, well, I've got to go," Chip said. "I'm tied up tomorrow, so I'll see you Saturday at seven. Oh," he added. "I can't wait to see those pearls on you."

After Brittany hung up, she leaned back against her pillow and stared at the ceiling. Chip was the one who was really nervous, she realized. He was obviously afraid that his parents wouldn't approve of his new girlfriend.

She knew exactly what would happen if they didn't—in about two days flat, Chip would find himself another girl and Brittany would be out of the picture. Maybe he'd even go back to his simpering Missy Henderson.

That wasn't going to happen, she told herself firmly. She went back to her dressing table and sat down. After all the time and energy and money she'd put into being the perfect girl for Chip, she wasn't going to let him slip away now. Even if she had to go to the library and check out a book on yachts, she'd make such a good impression on the Worthingtons that Chip would never let her go.

Fifteen minutes after Calvin left the store, Robin drank the last of the juice Lenny had brought. "I think I'll take off now," she said to Lenny. "I know it's five minutes early, but who's counting, right?"

Lenny looked across the store at Michael, who was busy with a customer. "Well," he said slowly, "I suppose it's okay, now that I've got the kid here."

"You're all heart, Lenny," Robin said with a laugh.

Robin was almost to the door when Michael spotted her. Excusing himself from the customer, he hurried over. "You're leaving?" he asked. "If you wait a couple of minutes, I'll walk with you."

Robin was tempted to say okay. It was just what Calvin deserved. But she decided that would be a rotten thing to do, to Cal and Michael both.

"Thanks, but I'm kind of in a hurry," she said as she kept on walking. "I'll see you tomorrow, Michael."

Calvin wasn't waiting outside Platters,

and it took Robin five minutes to find him. He was way down at the far end of the mall, staring into the window of a pizza shop.

"Is that what you'd rather have instead of ice cream?" she asked, walking up to him. "You don't have to talk me into it. I can always go for pizza."

Cal shrugged, not taking his eyes off the man spreading tomato sauce on pizza dough. "I'm not in the mood for pizza or ice cream," he said quietly.

"Hot dog?" Robin suggested.

Calvin shook his head and finally looked around. "Where's Mike?" he asked sarcastically. "I thought for sure you'd let him tag along."

"No," Robin said, just as sarcastically, "but if you'd like I'll go back and get him. At least he's not grumpy all the time."

"Very funny," Calvin said. "Wait until *his* girlfriend—if he ever has one of his own— starts flirting with some other guy and see how cheerful he is."

"Flirting?" Robin's dark eyes flashed angrily. "I have not been flirting with him, Calvin Roth, and you know it!"

"Oh, yeah? So how come every time I see you together you're always laughing and joking and he's always looking at you like he could die?"

"That's not my fault!" Robin almost shouted.

Several people turned their heads toward them. Robin lowered her voice. "It's not my fault Michael likes me," she said more quietly. "I haven't done a single thing to make him think I'm interested, either. I can't help it if he follows me around and asks me out—"

"Asks you out?" Calvin stared at her. "That kid actually asked you out?"

Robin sighed. She hadn't meant to tell him, but it was too late now. "Yes, he did," she said firmly.

"Huh." Cal shook his head in disgust. "So what did you say?"

Robin's anger flared again. "He didn't give me a chance to say anything, not that it's any of your business," she told him. "But for your information, I don't have any intention of going out with him. And I'm not so sure about *you* anymore, either!"

With that, Robin turned and stalked away.

Nikki was sprawled on her bed, trying to make sense out of the trig problems she had to do. But her mind kept drifting to what Ellen had told her—that Kevin had lost his key to Room 203. Ellen was really excited, and Nikki couldn't blame her. If Kevin was telling the truth, and Ellen was sure he was, then probably nobody on the student council was involved. Not that Nikki had really suspected any of them, anyway. That just left everybody else in the entire school, she thought with a sigh.

When her phone rang, Nikki grabbed it, glad for the interruption.

It was Nancy Drew. "Hi, Nikki. I just wanted to find out how everything's going with the money problem," she said.

"Well, we haven't caught anybody yet," Nikki said. "We're still keeping an extra-close watch on the room."

"Good," Nancy said. "It sounds like you're doing just about all you can without telling anybody else about it."

"Thanks, Nancy," Nikki said. "I'll tell Ellen, and I'll let you know as soon as anything happens. *If* anything happens," she added.

As soon as Nikki had finished talking with Nancy, the phone rang again.

"Hi," Niles said. "I was hoping I'd catch you."

"I'm glad you called," Nikki told him warmly. "What's up?"

"I just wanted to make sure we're still set for Saturday night."

"Sure we are," Nikki said. "I can't wait."

"Good." Niles sounded relieved. "Neither can I. We haven't been able to spend too much time together lately, it seems. And I'm eager to hear whatever big, dark secret it is you've promised to tell me."

Nikki smiled into the phone. "Well, it's not dark, and it won't be secret for much longer."

Niles laughed. "All right, I won't try to pry. I have to study now, but I thought I'd ask if we could eat lunch together tomorrow."

"Oh, I can't," Nikki said. Both Robin and Ellen had big tests the next day and needed every minute to study. Nikki had offered to spend her lunch watching the student council room.

"I'm—uh—I've got something I have to do."

"I see. All right, then," Niles said. "I'm sure I'll run into you sometime tomorrow."

"I hope so," Nikki told him.

After they'd said goodbye, Nikki sprawled on the bed again, thinking. She'd never worked up the nerve to come right out and ask Niles exactly how he felt about Gillian. But if Niles was madly in love with a girl in England, would he have sounded so disappointed that Nikki couldn't eat lunch with him?

That disappointment in Niles's voice was a good sign, Nikki decided, smiling into her trig book. When she told him she loved him, then maybe, just maybe, he'd tell her the same thing.

Robin was halfway through the parking lot when she realized she was going to have to walk home. She sure wasn't going to ride with Calvin, and she didn't want to wait for the bus. It was a long walk, but so what? Maybe by the time she got home, she'd be too tired to be mad anymore.

Just who did Calvin think he was, anyway? Her boss? Her owner? He acted as if she *belonged* to him! He'd actually accused her of flirting with Michael. As if it was her fault some other guy liked her!

By the time she was out of the huge parking lot and on the road, Robin was still seething. Kicking pebbles into the small piles of dirty snow along the road, Robin was so busy thinking up new names to call Calvin that she didn't notice Michael until he swerved in front of her on his bike.

"I shouted at you three or four times," he said breathlessly. "I guess you didn't hear me."

"Obviously," Robin snapped. Then she felt ashamed. There was no need to be mad at

Michael. He hadn't done anything wrong. "Sorry," she said. "I was just thinking hard."

"Not a good habit on a busy road," Michael said, adjusting his knit cap. "What happened to Cal? I thought he was taking you home."

"Something came up," Robin said shortly.

"Oh. Well, do you want a ride?"

Robin peered at his little mountain bike. "On that?"

"Oh. Right. Not too much room, is there?" He got off the bike. "How about if I walk with you?"

"Well, actually, Michael, I'd kind of like to be by myself," Robin said. "You know how it is when you're thinking about something."

"Oh, sure, I understand," he said quickly. He swung onto the bike and started pedaling away. After a few yards, he stopped, bracing himself on the ground with one foot.

When Robin walked up to him, he smiled nervously. "I know I told you there was no rush," he said. "But I was just wondering if—uh—you'd thought about—you know —maybe going out with me sometime?"

Robin studied him for a moment. It was time to tell him exactly how she felt. "Michael," she said softly, "I really like you. You're funny, you're smart, and you're nice.

But I don't want to go out with you. It's not you—it's me."

"Yeah," Michael said, his eyes lowered to the ground. "It's Calvin, too."

"What do you mean?"

"I mean, I know you're crazy about him," he said. "I could tell that from the second I saw you two together."

Robin didn't say anything.

Michael fiddled with the hand brakes, his eyes still on the ground. When he looked up, he was blushing. "I guess I made a pest out of myself, huh?"

"No," Robin said. Then she grinned. "Well, maybe just a little."

They both laughed. Then Michael raised his hand and tipped his hat to her. "Cal's a lucky guy, Robin. See you tomorrow at work, okay?"

# 11

Nikki's stomach was growling. Even with the crowd of kids walking by, laughing and shouting at each other, she could hear her stomach rumbling, "Feed me." Police officers always had doughnuts and coffee on stakeouts—why hadn't she brought something?

She'd come straight from her class to Room 203, skipping lunch. Now the smell of food from the cafeteria was drifting through the halls and driving her crazy. She dug in her bag, hoping to find a stick of gum or a hard candy. But all she came up with was a torn piece of cellophane from a chocolate cupcake she'd bought the day before. There weren't even any crumbs stuck to the cellophane.

She was near the water fountain. Maybe if she drank enough water, she could fool her stomach. She took a long drink. When she straightened up, she saw Karen and Ben walking toward her.

"Oh, please!" Nikki cried desperately. "One of you has to have something to eat! I'm starving!"

Ben laughed. "What's the matter, are you boycotting the cafeteria food?"

"No, I was just—waiting for somebody," Nikki said, feeling a little embarrassed. She wished she could tell him the whole truth.

"Niles, I bet," Ben said. "Listen, Karen and I are going to Leon's tomorrow night. Why don't you and Niles come, too?"

Karen smiled at Nikki. "It'd be fun."

"Oh, thanks, but Niles and I are eating at the club Saturday night," Nikki told them. "Another time, though, okay?"

"Great." Ben reached for Karen's hand, but she was busy rummaging in her bag.

A few seconds later Karen pulled out a package of peanut butter crackers. "They're a little mashed," she said, handing them to Nikki. "But they're still good—I only bought them yesterday."

Nikki thanked her gratefully. When Karen and Ben had walked on, she ripped open the package and wolfed down the crackers. She was gulping some more water when Robin came by, a book in one hand and an apple in the other.

"What's up?" Robin asked. "Anything interesting happening in Room 203?"

"Nothing," Nikki told her. "Nobody's gone in or out. What are you doing here, anyway?" she asked. "I thought you had a social studies test to cram for."

"I do. I couldn't concentrate, though, so I decided to take a break," Robin said. "But I'm not sure I'll learn much, anyway. I'm too mad to concentrate."

"What happened? Who are you mad at?" Nikki asked.

"Calvin." Robin sighed. "We had a huge fight yesterday. And I mean *major.*"

"What about?"

While Nikki kept one eye on the student council room, Robin quickly explained what had happened. "I haven't seen Calvin all morning," she finished. "And I hope I don't see him for the rest of the day. I'm not even sure I want to see him for a month!"

Nikki couldn't help smiling. "I don't believe that," she said. "You'd go bananas if you didn't see Cal for a month. No matter how mad you get, you're still crazy about him."

"Maybe," Robin admitted grudgingly. "But I can't help wondering if I'm totally stupid to be with a guy who gets jealous like that. Over nothing!"

"I guess it didn't seem like nothing to Cal," Nikki said. "Maybe he had trouble explaining how he felt and it just came out wrong."

"Maybe," Robin said again.

"So," Nikki said.

"So what?"

"So talk to Cal," Nikki urged. "And let *him* talk, too."

Robin tossed the apple up in the air a few times, thinking. As she caught it on the third toss, she said, "Do you want this? I'm not that hungry."

"I thought you'd never ask," Nikki said, eagerly reaching for the apple. "Thanks."

"Sure. I'd better go study now," Robin told her. "Catch you later, Nikki."

"Robin!"

Robin stopped walking and turned around.

"What are you going to do about Calvin?" Nikki asked.

"I guess you're right," Robin agreed. "I'll talk to him — in about a week, maybe!"

Nikki sighed and bit into the apple. Robin could be awfully stubborn sometimes. She hoped her friend wouldn't wait too long to talk with Calvin—both of them would be totally miserable after a few days of not speaking.

Still munching the apple, Nikki checked her watch. Lunch would be over soon. The hall was getting even more crowded with kids hurrying back to their lockers before their afternoon classes. So far, though, nobody was going into Room 203.

After five more minutes, Ellen came hurrying by. "I feel so guilty letting you hang out here during lunch, Nikki," she said. "But I just can't blow this test—I have to go study some more."

"It's all right, Ellen, really," Nikki assured her. "And I didn't miss lunch. I got a couple of handouts and I'm fine."

"Okay. I take it you haven't seen anything suspicious yet," Ellen said.

Nikki shook her head and Ellen sighed. "Try not to get down about it," Nikki told her. "I know it's hard, but we have to keep hoping the thief will slip up."

"I know," Ellen agreed. "But I'm really getting worried about the student council meeting next week. They're asking all the class treasurers to go over their account books. If we don't come up with the money, we'll have to cancel the big luau we were planning." She shook her head. "I'm even starting to dream about this."

"I talked to Nancy last night," Nikki said. "Do you think we should ask her to help? Maybe she could get in here over the weekend and check out the room."

Ellen bit her lip. If people found out Nancy Drew was checking something out at the school, the whole story could be revealed. But if nothing happened before next week's meeting, the story could come out, anyway. "All right," she agreed. "If we don't find anything out today, I guess we should ask her."

As Ellen hurried on to the library to study, Nikki gazed after her, feeling terrible. It just wasn't fair. Ellen had had such an awful time with kids over that rumor about her father. She shouldn't have to be going through this herself, too.

Finishing the apple, Nikki tossed it in a waste can and took another drink of water. When she straightened up this time, Niles was standing next to her.

Gulping down the swallow of water, Nikki smiled up at him. "I didn't think I'd see you till later," she said. "How'd you find me?"

"A brilliant deduction," Niles said with a laugh. "You have to admit, you've been spending a lot of time in this particular hallway."

"Oh." Nikki glanced over at the student council room. "I guess I have."

"Do you mind if I ask why?" Niles held up his hand. "I know. It's probably none of my business, but . . ." He shrugged and smiled at her. "I can't help asking."

"Well—" Nikki frantically tried to come up with a good reason for hanging out there. Why hadn't she done it before? "I just—" She stopped. "I can't tell you," she blurted out.

"I see." Niles stared at her for a minute. "Nikki, are you upset with me or something? You don't seem to be, but I can't help feeling that you've been trying to avoid me this week." He ran a hand over his hair and smiled again. "I know this may sound a bit conceited, but I can't think of any reason why you *should* be avoiding me."

"There isn't one!" Nikki cried. "Really, Niles, I'm not trying to avoid you at all."

"Well, I'm glad to hear that," Niles said, sounding somewhat relieved. "But I'm still curious about what's been keeping you glued to this spot."

"That's the part I can't tell you about," Nikki said. "You'll just have to trust me, though. It doesn't have anything to . . ."

Nikki's voice trailed off as she suddenly realized she'd been staring at Niles and not at the student council room. The hall had cleared out, too. She and Niles were the only ones in it. If anyone had gone into Room 203, she would have missed him or her.

"You were saying?" Niles said. "It doesn't have anything to do with whom? Me?"

Shaking her head, Nikki moved down the quiet hall until she came to the student council room. While a mystified Niles looked on, she reached out, took hold of the doorknob, and silently turned it. The door was still locked.

Somebody might have gone in and locked the door behind them, Nikki thought. She had about three more minutes until she had to get to class. She'd wait five and be a couple of minutes late. Maybe someone would come out. Of course, that someone might be totally innocent, but still . . .

"Nikki?" Niles broke into her thoughts. "Again, I hate to ask, but what is going on?"

Nikki moved away from the door. "Nothing, really," she said, walking back to the water fountain. "I was going to go in there and then I changed my mind." A really lame explanation, she thought. No wonder Niles was looking at her like she was crazy.

To cover her embarrassment, Nikki bent over the water fountain again. That's when she heard footsteps heading down the hall. She turned her head, the water cascading down her cheek, and saw Sasha Lopez moving toward them.

Sasha was searching for something in her big black carryall, so her head was down. Just before she reached the fountain, she glanced up. Seeing Nikki and Niles, she gave them a quick smile and spun around. As she turned, her shoulder bag caught on the handle of a locker. Suddenly, the entire contents of Sasha's bag were scattering across the tiled floor.

Niles stopped a rolling lipstick with his foot. "Here, let me help," he said. He picked up the lipstick and then reached for a package of gum that was skittering his way.

"No, that's all right," Sasha said quickly. "I can get it all."

"Don't be silly," Nikki said, wiping the

water off her cheek and crouching down to get Sasha's key chain.

"Please!" Sasha cried. "I can—"

But Nikki had already seen it—one of the keys on the chain had a strip of masking tape across the top. On the tape, written in black Magic Marker, was the number 203.

 **12**

Nikki's hand froze, inches from the key. She glanced up at Sasha and saw that her dark eyes were wide and frightened. All along, Nikki had known that somebody in the school had stolen the money. But now that she was face-to-face with the thief, she didn't know what to say or do. She'd thought she would be furious when and if they ever caught the mystery person. Instead, she felt surprised and very sad.

After what seemed like a long time, Nikki picked up the key chain and held it out to Sasha. "Here you go," she said, trying hard to keep her voice sounding casual.

Not looking at Nikki anymore, Sasha took

the keys and dropped them into her bag. "Thank you," she said, almost in a whisper. She turned and walked quickly down the hall and around the corner.

"That was strange," Niles said as Nikki stood up. "Sasha seemed awfully upset over such a small thing as dropping her bag, didn't she?"

"Mmmm," Nikki murmured. She was tempted to tell Niles the whole story right then, but first she had to talk to Ellen. As she and Niles started down the hall, Nikki kept thinking that there might be some reason why Sasha, who wasn't on the student council, had a key to Room 203. Deep down she knew, though, there was only one explanation. The expression in Sasha's eyes was as good as a confession.

After her last class Robin headed down the drive to the main street. She was trying to decide whether to walk to the mall or take the bus. The mall was pretty far, but she wasn't crazy about the bus. As she walked, she kept glancing over her shoulder at all the kids leaving in their cars, hoping to spot someone she could get a lift with. She hadn't seen Nikki all afternoon, and Nikki was probably watching the student council room anyway. But maybe Lacey hadn't left yet.

Lacey's mom was lending her her car so that Lacey could visit Rick after school.

The next time Robin looked back, she saw Calvin's car heading toward her. She looked straight ahead again and kept walking.

Ignoring the cars behind him, Calvin braked in the middle of the drive. He leaned over and opened the passenger door. "I know you're mad," he said. "But let's talk, anyway. If you're still mad when we're finished, I'll let you out and you can keep on walking."

Robin stared at him for a few seconds. Then, when a car honked loudly, she shrugged and jumped in beside Cal. Even if they fought, she decided, she'd get that much closer to the mall.

"Well?" Robin asked after they turned onto the street. "It was your idea to talk. You first."

Calvin glanced at Robin, then back at the road. "Okay," he said. "Here goes. First, I'm sorry. You were right. I was jealous about Michael and I was really dumb about the way I handled it."

"There was no reason to be jealous," Robin said quickly. "You should know that."

"I do know that, in my mind," Calvin told her. "But my feelings don't always listen to my mind. Anyway, Robin, what if things were reversed? What if some sophomore girl was crazy about me, following me everywhere, riding past my house? Wouldn't it bother you? Even though you knew I didn't care about her?"

"It probably would," Robin admitted. "But I don't think I'd be jealous. Plus, I wouldn't tell you what to do about it."

"Yeah, well, that's something else I wanted to talk about," Calvin said. He glanced into the rearview mirror, then pulled to the side of the road and stopped the car. "I can't talk about this and drive at the same time," he said. "Do you mind?"

Robin shook her head. She'd rather get to Platters late than in pieces. Besides, this was important.

"Okay," Calvin said again. "I know I came off really bossy and possessive, telling you to get rid of Michael."

"You sure did," Robin agreed.

"You know I'm not like that, though," Calvin added.

"That's why I got so mad," Robin told him. "You *aren't* like that, so why did you suddenly start acting that way?"

"I didn't mean to," Calvin said. "I just couldn't believe the way you treated the whole thing—like it was a joke."

"But it wasn't serious!" Robin cried. "How else was I supposed to treat it? It *was* kind of a joke."

"Not to me," Calvin said quietly. "And not to Michael, either."

Robin closed her eyes and thought about Michael Quinn. He had had a serious crush on her, she knew that. Maybe he still did. Even though she hadn't made fun of him or anything, maybe by not setting him straight right from the beginning, it seemed as though she had been teasing him. Or even leading him on a little.

Opening her eyes, Robin looked at Calvin. "Why didn't you tell me this before?" she asked. "I thought the whole thing was kind of funny, kind of nice, but I didn't mean to treat Michael like a joke. I wouldn't do that to somebody I liked. And I *do* like him, even if that makes you mad."

"That doesn't make me mad," Calvin said. "And I would have told you this before, but I was too mad at first to figure it out. Then, I couldn't seem to say it right. Every time I opened my mouth, it came out all wrong."

"Well, I'm glad you said it now," Robin told him. "It makes sense. I guess when I didn't take Michael's feelings seriously, you thought I might not take yours seriously, either." She reached out for Calvin's hand. "I guess we both messed up, huh?"

Calvin smiled and squeezed her hand. "It doesn't matter now. Even when I was so mad, I was still crazy about you."

Robin nodded. "That's what Michael said."

"What do you mean?"

"Well, he kept trying to pin me down about going out," Robin explained. "And I finally told him that I liked him, but he'd just have to find someone else to be his girlfriend. That's when he said he knew it all along. That we were crazy about each other, I mean."

Calvin leaned over and kissed Robin softly. Then, with his lips against her cheek, he whispered, "I guess maybe Mike's not so bad after all."

While Robin and Cal were working things out, Ellen was standing outside the art room, trying to work up her courage. She knew Sasha Lopez was inside. She'd seen her go in. Now Ellen had to go in, too, and confront her with what she knew.

Ever since Nikki had told her about the key in Sasha's bag, Ellen hadn't been able to think of anything else. What if Sasha denied taking the money? She'd had time to think up an excuse. And there was no way that Ellen could actually prove anything.

If that happens, Ellen told herself, if Sasha denies it, then you'll have to go to Ms. Rose or Mrs. Wolinsky or even the principal. But first, she wanted to talk to Sasha herself.

Taking a deep breath, Ellen pushed open the door to the art room. Several unfinished paintings stood on easels around the big bright room. In the center was a table where Ellen had once tried to sculpt a vase. It had come out lopsided, she remembered.

Sasha was at the table, pounding on a big lump of clay. She glanced at Ellen and smiled, a quick nervous smile. "I bet I know why you're here," she said.

"Yes, well . . ." Ellen started to say.

"Don't worry, I haven't forgotten," Sasha interrupted. "I've been thinking about it, I really have."

Ellen was puzzled. "You haven't forgotten?"

"Your sister's posters," Sasha reminded her with a laugh. "Don't tell me *you* forgot!"

"Oh. No, that's not what I—"

Still pounding on the lump of clay, Sasha interrupted again. "I saw that Suzanne put some up already," she said. "They're all right, but I don't think they say much about her. It's not too late to put up new ones. Maybe something a little bolder."

"Suzanne's not exactly bold," Ellen said. And neither am I, she thought. She had to say what she came to say. "Sasha, I didn't come to ask you about the posters."

"Oh?" Sasha took the clay and cut it in half on a wire that was stretched from a small pole to one corner of the table. She held up the two pieces and examined them. "Air holes," she said. "If I make something and bake it and don't get all the air pockets out, it'll explode in the oven."

Sasha went back to pounding the clay. Finally Ellen stepped closer to the table. Reaching out, she put her hand on top of Sasha's. "Sasha," she said, "Nikki told me you had a key to the student council room."

Ellen held her breath, waiting.

Slowly Sasha pulled her hand away, pushed the clay aside, and wiped her hands on a towel. Then she tossed her hair back and laughed. "She must have told you how I dropped my bag, too. It was so embarrassing. Have you ever had anything like that happen?"

Ellen nodded.

"Well, anyway, yes," Sasha went on, "I do have a key to that room. It's so funny—I found it the other week and I meant to give it to you or somebody on the student council, but I kept forgetting." She walked quickly across the room and took her bag from a wooden cubicle. She dug into the bag as she came back to the table. "Everything's all jumbled up since I dropped this," she muttered. "Here it is!"

Sasha brought out her key chain and unhooked the key to Room 203. "I'm glad you came by, Ellen," she said, holding out the key. "With my lousy memory, I probably would have carried this around for months before I remembered to give it back."

She's lying, Ellen thought as she took the key. Go ahead, she told herself, accuse her.

It was too late. Sasha was already heading for the door, her black skirt whirling around her slender legs. "I didn't realize how late it was," she said from the door. "I have to go, Ellen. Turn out the lights when you leave, will you?"

Without waiting for Ellen to answer, Sasha left the room.

Ellen didn't know what to feel. She leaned against the table, turning the key around and around in her hand. Why hadn't she accused her? Sasha was lying, Ellen knew she was. But somehow, she just couldn't bring herself to say it to her face.

Now she'd have to go to a faculty member, and everybody would wind up in the principal's office. Would Sasha lie then, too? If she did, there wouldn't be any way to prove it. It would be Ellen's word against hers.

The thought of a big scene made Ellen shudder. She knew she'd have to do something, but for the moment, she didn't feel like moving. She was still leaning against the table when the door opened and Sasha came back in.

Looking at her in surprise, Ellen saw that Sasha was crying. "Sasha?" she said.

"I couldn't do it," Sasha said, wiping her cheeks with her hands. "I've been going over that story all afternoon, and I thought I could go through with it. But I couldn't. You knew I was lying, didn't you?" she asked.

"Yes," Ellen said simply.

Sasha nodded and came to lean against the table next to Ellen. Taking a shaky breath, she said, "I did find the key. That part's true."

"What happened, Sasha?" Ellen asked quietly. "Why did you take the money? How did you even know it was there?"

"Oh, that was just an accident," Sasha said. "A lucky one, I thought. I found the key and went into the room to see if there was anyone inside I could give it to. Nobody was there, so I decided to put it in the desk drawer."

"The drawer I left the money in," Ellen said.

"Yes." Sasha wiped her eyes and took another shaky breath. "I don't know what happened to me!" she cried. "I've never stolen anything in my life!"

"Why this time?" Ellen asked. Her mind was racing. Sasha's family was hardly poor, she knew that. What could she possibly need to steal for?

"There's a special art class at the museum," Sasha explained. "I'm good in art, I love it, it's what I want to do with my life."

"Yes, I know," Ellen said. "But—"

"Well, my parents didn't want me to take the class," Sasha went on. "They think art's a nice hobby, but they want me to be a lawyer. They don't understand how serious I am about it. And they weren't going to pay two hundred dollars for an art class. I get all the art classes I need here at River Heights High, they said."

"And you didn't have enough to pay for it yourself?" Ellen asked.

Sasha nodded. "Oh, I have a part-time job at an art supply store." She laughed a little. "My parents don't like that, either. But, anyway, I didn't have enough saved. The museum wanted the full amount way before the class started. So when I saw that money lying there—I took it."

"And then you started putting it back," Ellen said.

"I felt so guilty, from the very second I took it," Sasha told her. "I haven't bought a single thing since then, not even lunch, trying to save every penny to pay it back." Her eyes filled with tears again and she sniffed.

Ellen took a packet of tissues out of her bag and handed it to her.

"Thanks," Sasha said, wiping her eyes and nose. "I know what you must think of me, Ellen. All I can say is, I'm really sorry. I'll talk to Mrs. Wolinsky and Ms. Rose right now, if you want. And I'll pay the money back. Every penny of it, I promise."

Ellen thought a minute. "Do you think you could pay it back by next week?"

"Not on what I make at the store," Sasha said. "I'll have to ask my parents to lend it to me. I was going to do that, anyway, so I could pay it back quicker."

"They'll be mad, won't they?"

"Will they ever!" Sasha blew her nose. "I want to tell them, though. Maybe they'll understand how much art means to me if they know I actually stole for it."

"Well, if you can really get the rest of the money by next week," Ellen said, "then I don't think anybody else needs to know about this."

Sasha stared at her in surprise. "You wouldn't tell? But why, Ellen? You must be furious with me!"

"I'm not, really," Ellen said. "Well, maybe a little. But, Sasha, I can tell how awful you feel right now, when only Nikki and I know about it. If the whole school finds out, you're going to feel a lot worse. I've been through that, remember? And so has Nikki."

"I remember," Sasha said softly.

"It's terrible, having people talk about you. And after you give the money back, people still won't trust you," Ellen said. "Not even if you never steal another cent in your life. I don't think you should have to go through that. I don't think it would be fair."

Sasha was quiet for a moment. Then she said, "I don't deserve it, but thank you, Ellen." She looked around the room. Suddenly, she ran over and grabbed a big sheet of white paper.

Flinging it down on one of the wooden tables, she took a Magic Marker out of her bag and started writing.

"Sasha, what are you doing?" Ellen asked.

"There's no way I can really thank you,"

Sasha said, still writing. "I mean, of course I'll pay the money back, but that's not enough. I want to do something—"

"Sasha, really, you don't—"

"There!" Sasha said. She held up the paper and turned it around so Ellen could see it. "For your sister," she said. "What do you think?"

Ellen looked at the paper. Across the top Sasha had written: "Suzanne Ming for Freshman Council." Under that were the words, "Honesty, Service, Excellence—A Family Tradition."

"What do you think?" Sasha asked again. "I mean, everybody knows what a good job you do as junior-class treasurer and on the student council. This'll make them think Suzanne will do a good job, too. I'm not sure about background color yet, but—"

"Sasha," Ellen interrupted with a smile. She felt as if a two-ton weight had been lifted from her back, and she was sure Sasha felt the same way. "It's wonderful," she said. "And I know Suzanne will like it. You couldn't have found a better way to thank me."

**13**

The dining room of the River Heights Country Club was elegant but cozy, with candles and small vases of flowers on the linen-covered tables. Black-coated waiters moved quietly around the room, taking orders and filling water glasses. Soft music played in the background, and the smell of delicious food wafted through the air.

The club was one of Brittany's favorite places, and normally she would have been enjoying herself. But not this night. This night she had to meet and impress Chip's parents. Even though she kept telling herself she'd do fine, she couldn't help being incredibly nervous. What if they hated her? What if all her spending and worrying turned out to be a waste?

"Well," Chip said, interrupting Brittany's thoughts. "They should be here soon. They must have gotten tied up at the Littons'. Mr. Litton just bought a yacht, too, so he and my dad are probably comparing notes."

Brittany smiled and took a sip of water. It had a paper-thin slice of lemon floating on the top, which kept bumping her lip. "I don't mind waiting," she said. The longer they had to wait, she thought, the less time she'd have to make conversation with the Worthingtons.

Surreptitiously, Brittany fished out the lemon slice and tucked it under the edge of her bread plate. As she took another sip of water, she saw Chip giving her a quick glance out of the corner of his eye. It was at least the tenth time he'd done it.

Nervously, she reached up and felt her hair. Had that short hunk come loose? Good, it was still in place. She'd spent at least forty-five minutes with her hair earlier, braiding the short part back and then twisting the rest of it up. She'd left a few curly tendrils hanging loose on her neck to keep the style from looking too much like a bun.

"Do I pass?" she asked Chip.

"Sure, you look just right," he said.

Just right for him or for his parents? Brittany wondered.

"There's just one thing," Chip said. "You're not wearing the pearls."

"Of course not," Brittany told him, reaching for her little black purse. "I wanted you to put them on." Actually, she hadn't dared put them on at home. Her parents would know how expensive they were, and there would have been a big scene while they discussed whether she could keep them.

"Here," Brittany said with a smile, holding the necklace out to him.

While Chip fumbled with the clasp, Brittany glanced around the dining room. Nikki Masters and Niles Butler were sitting at a table for two way on the far side. Nikki looked great, as usual, in a bright yellow dress and small gold earrings.

Glancing down at her own dark burgundy, Brittany sighed. She felt as if she blended right into the carpeting.

"So that's what's been happening," Nikki told Niles. "That's why I was spending so much time holding up the wall outside the student council room."

Niles had listened quietly to the story about the missing money. Now he whistled softly. "No wonder Ellen wanted to keep quiet about the whole thing," he said. "After what happened with her father, she must

have been scared to death of being suspected.''

"She was," Nikki said. "But, anyway, it's
all over now. Sasha's going to give back the
money, and everything will be fine. But,
Niles," she added, "don't say anything to
anyone, okay? Ellen said it was all right if I
told you, but if too many people find out, then
Sasha's reputation will be ruined."

"My lips are sealed," Niles assured her
with a smile. "I'm glad you told me, though.
Ever since you said you had a secret, I've
been dying to find out what it was."

Nikki reached for her butter knife and
almost dropped it. Should she tell him now?
Their table was private enough. Should she
lean close and tell him she loved him? Go on,
Nikki, she urged herself. Say it.

Just as Nikki was about to tell Niles how
she felt about him, the waiter arrived with
the salad cart. He started tossing lettuce and
grinding pepper two inches from the table.

Later, Nikki thought. You'll have plenty of
time to tell him later.

The atmosphere in Leon's was very different from the River Heights Country Club.
The place was packed with kids, loud with
music, and smelled of pizza and onion rings.

Robin and Calvin were sharing a large pie

with meatballs at a small table crammed between the jukebox and a video game. Neither of them cared about the crowding. The closer they were, the better, Robin decided.

In a booth at the back, Karen Jacobs and Ben Newhouse had just ordered cheeseburgers. After shrugging out of her jacket, Karen leaned across the table and touched Ben's hand. She was just beginning to feel comfortable enough with him to do things like that. "What are you thinking about?" she asked.

"Me?" Ben stopped scanning the room. "How can you tell I'm thinking about anything special?"

"Because whenever you are, you get these two little lines right between your eyebrows," Karen told him with a smile. "What is it? Something important?"

"No, I just——" Ben went back to checking out the room again. "I was thinking maybe we should ask Robin and Calvin to join us. They're really squeezed in over there."

Karen glanced over at them. "They look like they're having a great time," she said. "But if you want to ask them, it's fine with me."

Ben started to get up, then sat back down. "Maybe not," he said. "I'd rather be alone with you, anyway."

Karen's heart flipped a little when he said

that. Knowing Ben didn't want to share her with anyone made her feel fantastic. But why, she wondered, were those two little frown lines still there?

Brittany was trying to decide whether to eat a third roll when Chip suddenly slid back his chair and stood up. "There they are," he said, raising his hand and waving. "Mother, Dad! Over here!"

Forcing herself not to make any nervous, last-second adjustment to her hair, Brittany put on a welcoming smile and looked over at the couple that was heading toward the table.

Like Chip, Mr. Worthington was tall, square jawed, and brown haired. He had a winter tan, and walked across the room as if he owned it. He didn't look exactly friendly, Brittany thought. She hoped he was just hungry.

Then Brittany saw Chip's mother, and her eyes widened in shock. Mrs. Worthington's dark hair was pulled back, her burgundy cashmere dress had a slightly scooped neck and fell to just below her knees, and she was wearing a single strand of pearls.

Brittany couldn't believe it. Except for the difference in their ages, she and Mrs. Worthington could be twins.

\* \* \*

Now, Nikki told herself. The salad plates had been whisked away, and it would be a little while before the main courses came. She didn't want to wait any longer. She'd waited too long already.

Taking a deep breath, Nikki looked across the table at Niles. He was watching her, a smile on his face.

Before she had a chance to say anything, Niles reached over and touched her hand. "I've been meaning to tell you something," he said.

"Oh?" Maybe he was going to tell her first, Nikki thought. Maybe that was the reason for this romantic dinner.

"I got a letter today," he said.

"Oh." Okay, she thought. So he wasn't going to tell her he loved her.

"You remember Gillian, of course," Niles said. "Well," he went on, "I heard from her today, and she'll be arriving in River Heights soon."

Nikki's lips suddenly felt a little numb. "How soon is soon?" she managed to ask.

"Next week, as a matter of fact," Niles said. "I'm eager for you two to meet. Gillian's a great girl. I'm sure you'll like each other."

Nikki cracked a smile and drained her water glass. So much for telling him you love him, she thought. She couldn't tell him now. Not with Gillian coming. Maybe he loved Gillian. Maybe Nikki had just been a substitute for a while.

All she could do, Nikki decided, was wait and see. But it was going to be the longest wait of her life.

Across the dining room Brittany was listening, with what she hoped was an entranced expression, while Mr. Worthington talked on and on about his new yacht. *The Bitsy,* he had called it.

"She's a great little boat," Mr. Worthington said. "Thirty-four feet and sleek as a racehorse. We're going to take her out as soon as spring arrives, right, Chip?"

"Right, Dad," Chip said automatically.

"That's enough about your newest toy," Mrs. Worthington said, with an indulgent laugh.

Brittany couldn't have agreed more.

"Brittany," Chip's mother went on, "I've been admiring your necklace all through dinner. It's exquisite."

"Oh, thank you," Brittany said.

Chip beamed, but Brittany could tell he wasn't really smiling at her. He was smiling because he'd made her into the kind of girl his parents could approve of. Actually, she thought, the Worthingtons weren't so bad. As far as being snobs went, Chip was miles ahead of his parents. Brittany wondered if they knew what kind of creep their son really was.

Because Chip was definitely a creep. She'd known that all along, of course. But somewhere between the shrimp bisque and the palate-cleansing lemon sorbet, Brittany had decided she just couldn't keep up her act with him. If he had a decent personality and actually cared about her a little, she might have been able to. But spending a fortune on clothes? Wearing a dress and a hairstyle that made her look like his mother? Chip Worthington just wasn't worth it. She'd give the necklace back to him that very night, she decided.

"Brittany," Chip said, interrupting her thoughts. "Mother just asked if those pearls belong in your family."

"Oh, I'm sorry." Brittany smiled at Mrs. Worthington. "No, they don't," she said. "As a matter of fact, I borrowed this necklace for tonight only."

Chip's conceited smile disappeared, but before he could say anything, Brittany stuck the silver plate of after-dinner mints in his hands. "Here, Chip," she said with a sweet smile and a warning glance. "Suck on one of these."

At Leon's Ben finished the last bite of his cheeseburger and washed it down with soda. Then he put his chin in his hands and looked at Karen.

Karen felt her heart start to pound again. All he has to do is look at me, she thought, and I feel like flying. The little frown had disappeared and reappeared the whole time they'd been there. Now it was back.

"Okay," Karen said. "What is it? I know something's on your mind, so why don't you tell me?"

"You're right," Ben said. "Something *is* on my mind and I just can't get used to it."

"Well, what is it?" Karen asked again. She couldn't tell what Ben was feeling. Nervous? Excited? Maybe both. "Has something happened?"

"You could say that." Ben cleared his throat. "I got a letter from Emily today," he said. "Things aren't working out very well in New York, and her series is being canceled. She's moving back to River Heights to live with her dad for a while."

Karen had a sudden picture in her mind of Emily Van Patten — tall, willowy, drop-dead gorgeous, and blond. Ben had been crazy about her, and they'd gone together for ages. Karen thought Emily was out of their lives for good. Now it seemed she was coming back.

"Well," Karen said faintly. "That's really a surprise."

"It sure is," Ben agreed. "I've been kind of numb ever since I got the letter."

Karen was anything but numb. She was disappointed and scared, and she wished she'd never asked Ben what was on his mind. With Emily Van Patten back in town, where would that leave *her*?

———————

The return of Emily Van Patten spells disaster for Karen when Ben decides he wants to start dating his old girlfriend again. But when he wants to keep seeing Karen, too, the trouble really begins. Meanwhile, Niles's old girlfriend has arrived. Gillian is gorgeous and talented, and Niles can't take his eyes off her. Is this the end of romance for Nikki and Karen? Find out in River Heights #11, *Broken Hearts.*